Samuel French Acting Edition

Saint Joan

by George Bernard Shaw

adapted with additional scenes
by Chelsea Marcantel

be invented, including mechanical, electronic, photocopying, recording, videotaping, or otherwise, without the prior written permission of the publisher. No one shall upload this title(s), or part of this title(s), to any social media websites.

For all enquiries regarding motion picture, television, and other media rights, please contact Concord Theatricals Corp.

MUSIC USE NOTE

Licensees are solely responsible for obtaining formal written permission from copyright owners to use copyrighted music in the performance of this play and are strongly cautioned to do so. If no such permission is obtained by the licensee, then the licensee must use only original music that the licensee owns and controls. Licensees are solely responsible and liable for all music clearances and shall indemnify the copyright owners of the play(s) and their licensing agent, Concord Theatricals Corp., against any costs, expenses, losses and liabilities arising from the use of music by licensees. Please contact the appropriate music licensing authority in your territory for the rights to any incidental music.

IMPORTANT BILLING AND CREDIT REQUIREMENTS

If you have obtained performance rights to this title, please refer to your licensing agreement for important billing and credit requirements.

SAINT JOAN was first produced by the Delaware Theatre Company (Bud Martin, Executive Director; Matt Silva, Managing Director) in Wilmington, Delaware on February 6, 2019. The performance was directed by Bud Martin, with sets by Colin McIlvaine, costumes by Millie Hiible, lights by Thom Weaver, sound by Michael Kiley, projections by Nick Hussong and Joey Moro, and fight choreography by Sean Michael Bradley. The production stage manager was Alison Hassman. The cast was as follows:

JOAN . . . . Clare O'Malley

ST. MARGARET. . . . . .Mary Toumanen

ST. CATHERINE . . . . .Tai Verley

LADY WARWICK / HOUSEKEEPER / BARONESS / ABBESS . . . .
. . . . Mary Martello

ARCHBISHOP / INQUISITOR / MESSENGER. . . . . .Dan Kern

CHARLES / STOGUMBER / D'ESTIVET . . . . Michael Doherty

BISHOP CAUCHON / DE BAUDRICOURT / BLUEBEARD / LIEUTENANT. . . .
. . . . .Charlie DelMarcell

DUNOIS / POULENGEY / PAGE / LADVENU. . . . . . . Sean Michael Bradley

SAINT JOAN was adapted on commission from Delaware Theatre Company.

CHARACTERS

ACTRESS 1 – (20s) A serious, passionate young peasant girl driven by divine inspiration to lead an army against the British occupiers of France; also wrestles with moments of deep self-doubt and fear; plays **JOAN**, our protagonist.

ACTRESS 2 – (40s-60s) Sharp, calculating, self-serving; plays **HOUSEKEEPER, BARONESS, ABBESS, LADY WARWICK**.

ACTRESS 3 – (20s) Comforting, brilliant, a scholar, historically Egyptian; plays **SAINT CATHERINE** of Alexandria.

ACTRESS 4 – (20s) Quiet but fierce, ancient, historically Mediterranean/Greek; plays **SAINT MARGARET** of Antioch.

ACTOR 1 – (20s-40s) Spineless, fickle, sometimes ridiculous, but smart; plays **CHARLES THE DAUPHIN, CHAPLAIN STOGUMBER, PROSECUTOR D'ESTIVET**.

ACTOR 2 – (40s-60s) Wise, careful, and cold; plays **ARCHBISHOP OF RHEIMS, LEMAÎTRE THE INQUISITOR**, a **MESSENGER** from the future.

ACTOR 3 – (20s-40s) Dashing and loyal, but plays "by the book" to a fault; plays **BERTRAND DE POULENGEY**, a **PAGE**, **DUNOIS** Bastard of Orléans, Brother **LADVENU** a Dominican monk

ACTOR 4 – (20s-40s) Outrageous, comic, and cruel; plays **ROBERT DE BAUDRICOURT, BLUEBEARD**, a French **LIEUTENANT, BISHOP CAUCHON**

SETTING

War-torn France and England

TIME

The Fifteenth Century

THE SCENES

Prologue	Vaucouleurs, February 1429
Scene One	Vaucouleurs, February 1429
Scene Two	Chinon, April 1429
Interlude One	Sainte-Catherine-de-Fierbois, April 1429
Scene Three	Loire River, April 1429
Scene Four	An English Castle, May 1429
Coronation Moment	Rheims Cathedral, July 1429

Intermission

Scene Five	Rheims Cathedral, July 1429
Interlude Two	Beaurevoir Castle Keep, June 1420
Scene Six	Rouen, May 1431
Epilogue	Paris, 1456

Appendix – Timeline of Historical Events

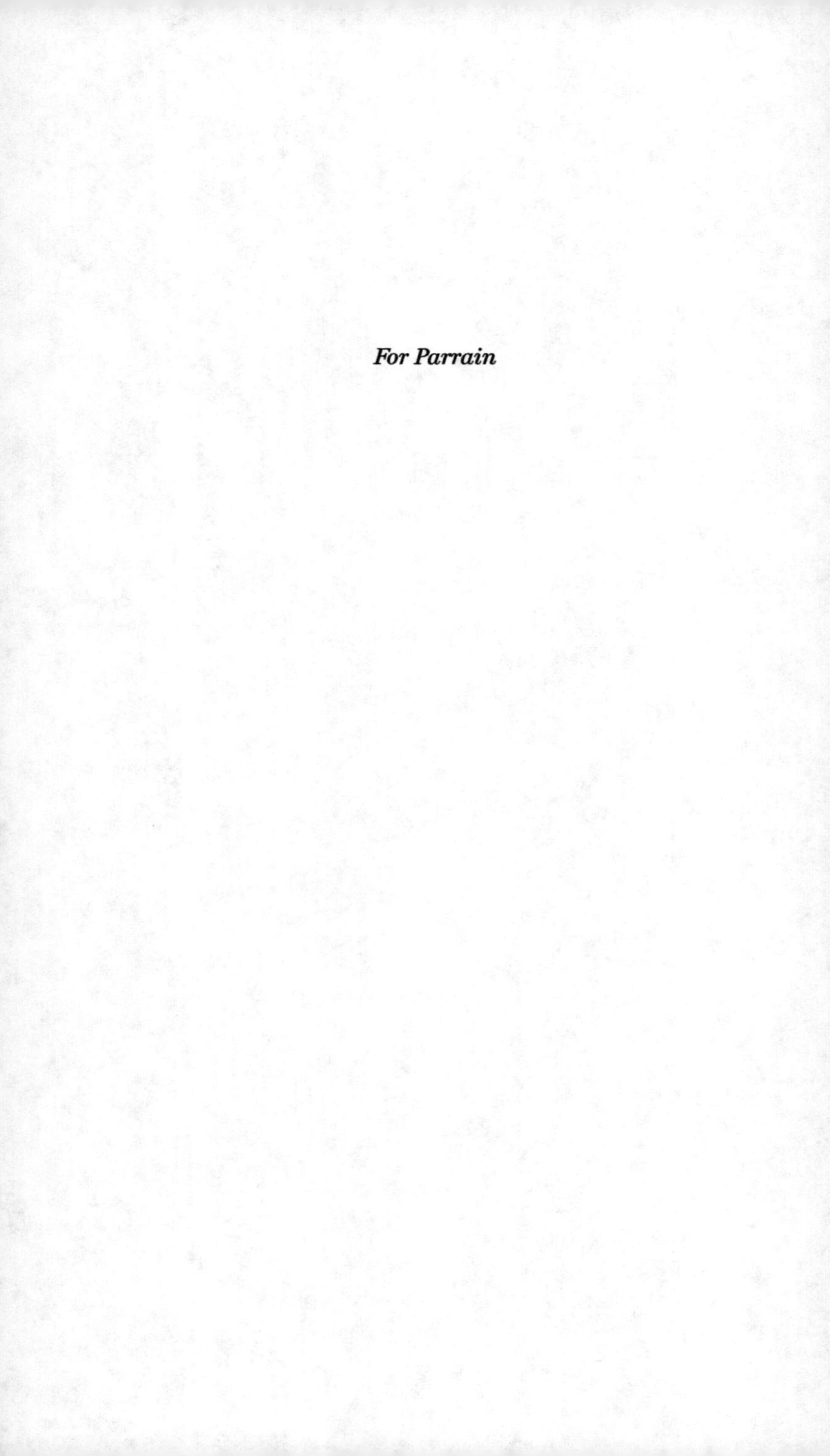

For Parrain

Prologue

(Lights up on a courtyard in the castle of Vaucoulers on a fine spring morning in 1429.)

*(**JOAN**, a serious, mature farm girl of seventeen, paces like a caged animal in front of a closed door. She has requested an audience with the lord of the castle, but has not been allowed up. This has been going on for days.)*

(When she is finally granted admission, she will initiate a series of events that will lead to the defeat of the English army, the coronation of the French king, and her own trial and death.)

JOAN. *(Fuming.)* Again today he will not see me! Have I come all this way from home to be defeated by a DOOR? What good is a divine plan, set on from God himself, if the first petty little man I meet can derail it?

*(**JOAN** is alone for a moment, then she is joined by **ST. CATHERINE**, a comforting and confident Egyptian woman, and **ST. MARGARET**, a quiet but fierce Mediterranean woman. Both are virgin martyrs, aged seventeen.)*

You promised he would help me.

ST. MARGARET. Just because your path is divinely set does not mean you won't encounter obstacles.

ST. CATHERINE. You will face much resistance, every step of the way.

JOAN. An illiterate farm girl who can't even manage an audience with her local lord. Are you sure I'm the one you mean to call to this effort?

ST. CATHERINE. If not you, who?

ST. MARGARET. It must be you, and it must be now. The time has come to begin your great work.

JOAN. Tell that to the man in the tower.

ST. CATHERINE. Beloved Jehanne, the King of Heaven sees your doubt and impatience, but pledges that he will be with you forever, as he has always been. France needs you.

JOAN. But no one will listen to me! Why should powerful men listen to a teenage girl who knows nothing of warfare, nothing of the world?

ST. MARGARET. Whether or not they believe you does not change the fact that you are right. Your job is not to convince them, it is to tell the truth, no matter the consequences.

ST. CATHERINE. You must be persistent. And patient. You are the chosen vessel. And we will be right beside you.

ST. MARGARET. We have shown you visions of the victories you will claim, the coronation in the Cathedral at Rheims, and beyond. The manifestation of your visions begins in this instant.

JOAN. *(Lashing out.)* Yes, yes, I have seen my beautiful armor and my beautiful horse and all the beautiful men I will lead under my banner. Isn't vanity a sin? Isn't pride?

ST. MARGARET. *(Suddenly awful and terrible to behold.)* You doubt our counsel now? After three years of preparation?!

> (**JOAN** *cowers before the ancient divine.*
> **ST. CATHERINE** *steps in to soothe them both.)*

ST. CATHERINE. *(Gently.)* You are right, beloved. It would be sinful to seek glory for Jehanne. But you will not. Your heart is too pure. You will seek glory for the Almighty, and through that, peace for France.

ST. MARGARET. Search your intentions, and quiet your soul.

ST. CATHERINE. *(Soothingly.)* We know that you are being asked to shoulder a great burden, Jehanne. Your heart will be broken, your faith will be tested, and every step you take will bring you closer to calamity – starting today. But in the end, your soul will be glorified and God's Will will be done.

JOAN. *(Quietly.)* I believe what you say. I am afraid that I will falter.

ST. CATHERINE. You will falter many times. But we will be with you. I was afraid, when they put me on the torture wheel to break me.

ST. MARGARET. I was afraid, when the headsman came toward me with the ax. It is human to be afraid, Jehanne.

JOAN. Yes?

ST. CATHERINE. Yes. You are afraid. But you will never be alone.

> (**JOAN** *looks back up at the tower and the closed door.*)

JOAN. What good is all the courage in the world in the face of this bureaucracy?

ST. MARGARET. It is not the men in the towers who will save France. It is the men in the fields, in the villages, in the stables. And you.

ST. CATHERINE. Go and speak with the soldiers. Win them to your cause. Tell them God is on their side.

JOAN. Oh, everybody says things like that.

ST. CATHERINE. Yes, but you believe it. And that will make all the difference to them.

ST. MARGARET. Act, and God will act.

> (*Lights dim on the courtyard.*)

Scene One

(Lights up on the castle of Vaucoulers, a few days later...)

*(**CAPTAIN ROBERT DE BAUDRICOURT**, a military squire and petty tyrant, is storming terribly at his weary **HOUSEKEEPER**, who is used to this kind of abuse.)*

DE BAUDRICOURT. No eggs! No eggs!! Thousand thunders, woman, what do you mean by no eggs?

HOUSEKEEPER. Sir: it is not my fault. It is the act of God.

DE BAUDRICOURT. Blasphemy. You tell me there are no eggs; and you blame your Maker for it?

HOUSEKEEPER. What can I do? I cannot lay eggs.

DE BAUDRICOURT. And now you jest about it.

HOUSEKEEPER. We all have to go without eggs just as you have, sir. The hens will not lay.

DE BAUDRICOURT. Indeed! Now listen to me, you.

HOUSEKEEPER. Yes, sir?

DE BAUDRICOURT. What am I?

HOUSEKEEPER. What *are* you, sir?

DE BAUDRICOURT. Yes: what am I? Am I Robert, Squire of Baudricourt and captain of this castle of Vaucouleurs; or am I a cowboy?

HOUSEKEEPER. *(Indulging him.)* Oh, sir, you know you are a greater man here than the king himself.

DE BAUDRICOURT. Precisely. And now, do you know what you are?

HOUSEKEEPER. *(Sarcastically.)* I am nobody, sir, except that I have the honor to be your housekeeper.

DE BAUDRICOURT. *(Enraged by her making fun of him.)* You have not only the honor of being my housekeeper, but the privilege of being the worst, most incompetent, driveling sniveling jibbering jabbering idiot of a housekeeper in all of France.

HOUSEKEEPER. *(Standing her ground.)* To a man like you I must seem like that, yes.

DE BAUDRICOURT. *(Backing off a little.)* My three Barbary hens and the black are the best layers in Champagne. And you come and tell me that there are no eggs! Who stole them? The milk was short yesterday, too: do not forget that.

HOUSEKEEPER. I know, sir. I know only too well. There is no milk: there are no eggs: tomorrow there will be nothing.

DE BAUDRICOURT. Nothing! You will steal the lot, eh?

HOUSEKEEPER. Nobody is stealing anything. We are bewitched.

DE BAUDRICOURT. Bewitched?! Robert de Baudricourt burns witches and hangs thieves. No. Unacceptable. You bring me four dozen eggs and two gallons of milk here in this room before noon, or Heaven have mercy on your bones!

HOUSEKEEPER. You can do whatever you like to my bones. I tell you there are no eggs, and there will be none – not as long as The Maid is at the door.

(**DE BAUDRICOURT** *stares at her blankly.)*

The girl from Lorraine, sir. From Domrémy. She asked for an audience with you two days ago, and you denied her.

DE BAUDRICOURT. Do you mean to say that that impudent girl is here still? I told you to send her back to her father with my orders to give her a good hiding.

HOUSEKEEPER. I have told her to go, sir. She won't.

DE BAUDRICOURT. I did not tell you to tell her to go: I told you to throw her out. Why do I keep fifty men-at-arms and heaps of able-bodied servants if no one will carry out my orders? Are you afraid of her?

HOUSEKEEPER. She is so...positive, sir.

DE BAUDRICOURT. *(Suddenly grabbing her arms.)* Positive! Now see here. I am going to throw you downstairs.

HOUSEKEEPER. Please don't.

DE BAUDRICOURT. Well stop me by being positive! Apparently, any whore of a girl can do it.

HOUSEKEEPER. Sir: you cannot get rid of *her* by throwing *me* out. She wants to go and be a soldier herself. She wants you to give her soldier's clothes. Armor, sir! And a sword, too. She says she will not go without them. And I believe we shall have no eggs or milk until she has what she wants.

> (**DE BAUDRICOURT** *lets his* **HOUSEKEEPER** *go, then thinks for a moment.*)

DE BAUDRICOURT. I see I'll have to handle this myself. A grown woman afraid of a simpering little peasant girl.

HOUSEKEEPER. She doesn't simper, sir. She is rough, but she really doesn't seem to fear anything.

DE BAUDRICOURT. *(Grimly.)* She will fear me. *(Pause.)* Where is she now?

HOUSEKEEPER. Down in the courtyard, sir, talking to the soldiers. She is always talking to the soldiers except when she is praying.

DE BAUDRICOURT. Praying! Ha! You believe she prays? I know the sort of girl that is always talking to soldiers. She shall talk to me a bit.

> *(He goes to the window and shouts.)*

You there!

JOAN. *(Offstage.)* Is it me, sir?

DE BAUDRICOURT. Yes, you.

JOAN. *(Offstage.)* Are you the Captain?

DE BAUDRICOURT. Yes, damn your impudence, I'm the Captain. Come up here. Quick!

> (**JOAN** *appears in the doorway. She is eager and full of hope –* **DE BAUDRICOURT**'s *scowl does not check or frighten her in the least.*)

JOAN. *(Bobbing a curtsey.)* Good morning, Captain Squire. You are to give me a horse and armor and some soldiers, and send me to the Dauphin. Those are your orders from my Lord.

ROBERT. *(Outraged.)* MY ORDERS?! And who the devil is your lord? Go back to him and tell him that I take no orders except from the king.

JOAN. *(Reassuringly.)* My Lord is the King of Heaven.

DE BAUDRICOURT. Oh. Okay. The girl's mad.

JOAN. Everyone says I am mad until I talk to them, Squire. You will see that it is the will of God that you are to do what He has put into my mind.

DE BAUDRICOURT. Well, I think it is the will of God that I send you back to your father with orders to thrash the madness out of you. What have you to say to that?

JOAN. You say that now, Squire, but you will find it all turns out quite different. For two days you said you would not see me, but here I am.

DE BAUDRICOURT. *(Feeling that he has lost ground.)* Now listen to me. I am going to assert myself.

JOAN. Oh please do, Squire. It *is* your house. *(Short pause.)* Now, the horse will cost sixteen francs. It is a good deal of money, I know, but I shall not want many soldiers, to start. The Dauphin will give me all I need to end the siege of Orléans.

DE BAUDRICOURT. *(Flabbergasted.)* The siege of Orléans has been ongoing for six months!

JOAN. Yes. And God has sent me to end it, and win victory for France. Three men will be enough for you to send if they are good men and gentle to me. Polly and Jack have promised to come with me –

DE BAUDRICOURT. *(Interrupting.)* "Polly"! You impudent baggage, you dare call Squire Bertrand de Poulengey "Polly" to my face?

JOAN. *(Continuing.)* I think John Godsave will come, and Dick the Archer, and their servants John of Honecourt and Julian. There will be no trouble for you, Squire: I have arranged it all: you have only to give the order.

DE BAUDRICOURT. *(Amazed.)* Well, I'll be damned!

JOAN. *(Sweetly.)* Oh no: God is very merciful.

>*(The* HOUSEKEEPER *snickers.)*

And the blessed saints Catherine and Margaret, who speak to me every day, will intercede for you. Your name will be remembered forever as my first helper.

DE BAUDRICOURT. *(To his* HOUSEKEEPER.*)* Is this true about the men she names?

HOUSEKEEPER. Yes, sir. They want to go with her.

DE BAUDRICOURT. *(Crossing to the window, then calling down.)* Monsieur de Poulengey, come up to me!

HOUSEKEEPER. Think of those hens, sir, the best layers in Champagne; and –

DE BAUDRICOURT. *(Interrupting.)* Think of my boot; and take your backside out of reach of it. Get out of my sight! *(To* JOAN, *pointing at the door.)* You. Wait outside.

JOAN. Yes, sir. Only please be as quick as you can. I need to make my way to the court of the Dauphin with all haste. I must be with him before mid-Lent, though I wear my legs to the knees on the road.

>(JOAN *leaves the room, followed by the* HOUSEKEEPER.*)*

>(BERTRAND DE POULENGEY *enters. He is a quiet and thoughtful gentleman, a perfect contrast to the blustering, self-assertive* DE BAUDRICOURT. DE POULENGEY *salutes and awaits orders.)*

DE BAUDRICOURT. At ease, Polly. Sit down. Let's have a friendly chat.

>(DE POULENGEY *sits.* DE BAUDRICOURT *softens his tone.)*

Polly, I'm going to speak to you now like a father. It's about this girl you are interested in. Now, I have seen her. I have talked to her. First, she's mad. That doesn't matter. Second, she's not a farm wench. She's a bourgeoise. That matters a good deal. Her father is a farmer, but still, he might have a cousin who's a lawyer, or in the Church. No doubt it seems to you a very simple thing to take this girl away – tricking her into the belief that you are taking her to the Dauphin – and do what you will with her. But if you get her into trouble, you'll get me into no end of a mess, as I am her father's lord, and responsible for her protection. So, Polly, hands off her.

DE POULENGEY. I should as soon try to put my hands on the Blessed Virgin herself, as this girl.

DE BAUDRICOURT. But she says you and Jack and Dick have offered to go with her. What for? You're not going to tell me you take her seriously.

DE POULENGEY. There is something about her – and it hasn't anything to do with her being a woman. She is hasty and fearless and she makes us want to move. The guards have stopped swearing in front of her. The men are inspired.

DE BAUDRICOURT. Oh, come, Polly! Common sense was never your strong point; but this is too much.

DE POULENGEY. What is the good of common sense? If we had any at all, we would surrender. The war is in its ninetieth year, the extinction of France is at hand. The English invaders have completed their lines around Orléans, and the city starves. The French cavalry is defeated at every turn, our ranks thinned, our spirits crushed. A foreign king is proclaimed in Paris, and foreign armies of skilled fighters occupy our lands. And worse for France, worse even than the fierceness of her enemies, are the vices and crimes of her own children. Many of our nobles, our prelates, and our magistrates have sworn their loyalty to the English king. The lives of the poor in France, amid all this anarchy and terror, are wretched beyond the power of language. The wolves are at the door. You feel them, don't you? I tell you that nothing can save our side now but a miracle.

DE BAUDRICOURT. Miracles are all well and good, Polly. The only difficulty about them is that they don't happen nowadays.

DE POULENGEY. I used to think so. I am not so sure now.

DE BAUDRICOURT. Oh! You think the girl can work miracles, do you?

DE POULENGEY. I think the girl herself is a bit of a miracle. *(Short pause.)* Anyhow, she is the last card left in our hand. Better to play her than throw up the game.

DE BAUDRICOURT. *(Giving him up.)* You are as mad as she is.

DE POULENGEY. We need a few mad people now. See where the sane ones have landed us! Perhaps she can infect the soldiers at Orléans the way she has infected me, and they will take back the city. *(Pause.)* I will conduct her to the Dauphin – unless you stop me. The responsibility falls on you, whichever way you decide.

DE BAUDRICOURT. You don't see how awkward this is for me. And horses aren't cheap!

DE POULENGEY. I will pay for her horse.

DE BAUDRICOURT. *(Calling to the doorway.)* Girl! Get in here!

> *(**JOAN** re-enters.)*

What is your name?

JOAN. My parents named me Jeahnette. In Lorraine, they called me Jehanne. The soldiers call me The Maid.

DE BAUDRICOURT. Your surname, girl, what is your surname?

JOAN. My father sometimes calls himself d'Arc.

DE BAUDRICOURT. How old are you?

JOAN. Seventeen.

DE BAUDRICOURT. What did you mean when you said that Saint Catherine and Saint Margaret talk to you every day?

JOAN. Just what I said.

DE BAUDRICOURT. What are they like?

JOAN. *(Suddenly obstinate.)* I will tell you nothing about that: they have not given me leave.

DE BAUDRICOURT. But you actually see them; and they talk to you just as I am talking to you?

JOAN. No. And yes. I cannot make you understand. I hear voices telling me what to do. They come from God.

DE BAUDRICOURT. They come from your imagination.

JOAN. Of course. That is how the messages of God come to us.

DE POULENGEY. Checkmate.

DE BAUDRICOURT. No fear! No fear in her at all.

JOAN. I have a great many fears, sir. But my orders overrule them. Far rather would I sit and sew beside my poor mother, for fighting is not of my condition. But I must fight, because my Lord will have it so.

DE BAUDRICOURT. Your orders are to raise the siege of Orléans?

JOAN. And to make the English leave France. And to crown the Dauphin in Rheims Cathedral. Then we will have peace.

DE BAUDRICOURT. *(Sarcastic.)* Oh is that all?

JOAN. *(Charming.)* For now. But I'm open to future endeavors once those are completed.

DE BAUDRICOURT. I suppose you think raising a siege is as easy as chasing a cow out of a meadow. Have you ever seen English soldiers fighting? Have you ever seen them plundering, burning, turning the countryside into a desert?

JOAN. *(Darkly.)* I come from a peasant village without military guard. I have seen English soldiers fighting, and much, much worse.

DE BAUDRICOURT. But you believe you'll be able to stop them?

JOAN. They are only men. God made them just like us; but He gave them their own country and their own language and their own king. It is not His will that they should come into our country and try to rule us.

DE BAUDRICOURT. Who has been putting such nonsense into your head? Don't you know that most people don't care at all? Soldiers must fight and citizens must pay taxes. Everyone is subject to their feudal lord, and it matters nothing to them whether he is the king of England or the king of France.

JOAN. We are all subject to the King of Heaven; and He gave us our languages and our homes. I believe that the English should have a home – but not by taking ours. And they should have a king – but so should France. God has blessed the blood royal in France as surely as he has in England.

DE BAUDRICOURT. We are not talking about God: we are talking about the real world.

JOAN. You must not be afraid, Robert –

DE BAUDRICOURT. *(Interrupting.)* Damn you, I am not afraid. And who gave you leave to call me Robert?!

JOAN. Listen to me, Robert. At Domrémy we had to fly to the next village to escape from the English soldiers. Yes, I have seen them fighting, and stealing, and burning. They have not half my strength.

DE BAUDRICOURT. Do you know why they are called *goddams*?

JOAN. No. Everyone calls them *goddams*.

DE BAUDRICOURT. It is because they are always calling on God to condemn their souls to perdition. That is what "goddam" means in their language. How do you like it?

JOAN. God will be merciful to them, and they will act like His good children when they go back to the country He made for them. When all this bloodshed and destruction is over. God will be merciful to us all.

DE BAUDRICOURT. Your sword, Polly.

(**DE POULENGEY** *hands over his sword.*)

(*Handing the sword to* **JOAN.**)

Can you even lift this?

JOAN. *(Lifting the sword easily and pointing it at him.)* I've been working in the fields since I could walk. I'm very strong.

DE BAUDRICOURT. Impressive. Now show me some sword work.

> **(JOAN** *looks uncertainly at* **DE POULENGEY,** *who nods supportively.)*

Come on, girl. Come at me!

> **(JOAN** *begins to take large, clumsy swings with the sword, which* **DE BAUDRICOURT** *sidesteps easily.)*

You believe you will drive the English from France? You can't even drive me from this room, and I am unarmed.

JOAN. Sword skills can be taught! Any stage actor can learn them.

DE BAUDRICOURT. Who will teach you?

DE POULENGEY. I will, sir.

JOAN. You see? God provides. And I have what cannot be taught, what our soldiers have lost: certainty that we will triumph.

DE BAUDRICOURT. *(Wearily.)* The English will take Orléans. You cannot stop them, nor ten thousand like you.

JOAN. Ten like me can stop them with God on our side. *(Growing impatient.)* You don't understand, Robert. Our soldiers are always beaten because they are fighting only to save their skins. Our knights are thinking only of the money they will make in English ransoms. But I will teach them all to fight that the will of God may be done in France, to fight for peace, for their families, for their homes, for their fellow citizens. And then they will drive the English before them like sheep.

DE BAUDRICOURT. This war has been going on for nearly a century.

JOAN. Yes. And I was born to end it. Now give me armor and a horse.

DE BAUDRICOURT. *(To* **DE POULENGEY.***)* This may be all rot, Polly, but the Dauphin might swallow it. And if she can put fight into <u>him</u>, she can put it into anybody.

DE POULENGEY. I can see no harm in trying. Can you?

DE BAUDRICOURT. *(Turning to* **JOAN.***)* Now you listen to me, and don't cut in before I have time to think.

JOAN. Yes, Squire.

DE BAUDRICOURT. Your orders are, from me, that you are to go to the Dauphin at Chinon, under the escort of this gentleman and his friends.

JOAN. Oh, Squire! Your head is all circled with light, like a saint's.

DE POULENGEY. How is she to get into the royal presence?

DE BAUDRICOURT. I don't know: how did she get into my presence? If the Dauphin can keep her out he is a stouter man than I take him for.

JOAN. And the armor? I may have a soldier's armor, mayn't I, Squire?

DE BAUDRICOURT. Have what you please. Take the whole damn stable. I wash my hands of it.

JOAN. *(Wildly excited.)* Come, Polly.

DE BAUDRICOURT. Goodbye, Polly. I am taking a big chance. Few other men would have done it. But as you say, there is something about her.

> *(Shaking* **DE POULENGEY***'s hand.)*

Go, and come what may.

> *(***JOAN** *exits, followed by* **DE POULENGEY**.*)*

> *(***ROBERT**, *still very doubtful whether he has not been made a fool of, scratches his head and slowly comes back from the door.)*

> *(The* **HOUSEKEEPER** *runs in with a basket.)*

HOUSEKEEPER. Sir, sir –

DE BAUDRICOURT. What now?

HOUSEKEEPER. The hens are laying like mad, sir. Five dozen eggs!

DE BAUDRICOURT. *(Crossing himself.)* Christ in heaven!

> *(Taking the eggs.)*

Almost miraculous.

> *(Lights dim on the room.)*

Scene Two

(March 1429.)

(The Dauphin's court in exile at Chinon, in Touraine. An antechamber has been created using curtains to section off a part of the larger throne room.)

*(The **ARCHBISHOP** of Rheims, an imposing prince of the church, waits for the Dauphin to arrive.)*

*(A **PAGE** enters and the **ARCHBISHOP** looks at him expectantly.)*

THE PAGE. No, my lord: it is not His Majesty. The Baron de Rais is approaching.

ARCHBISHOP. Young Bluebeard! Why announce *him*?

*(The **PAGE** bows and exits.)*

*(**BLUEBEARD** enters. He is a nobleman and a soldier whose predominant characteristic is a kind of forced extravagance and gaiety (and who will, a dozen years hence, confess to the murders and abuse of hundreds of children, and be hanged).)*

BLUEBEARD. *(Swanning up to the **ARCHBISHOP** with an exaggerated bow.)* Your faithful lamb, Archbishop.

ARCHBISHOP. Good day, Baron.

*(They wait in uncomfortable silence for just a moment, before **BLUEBEARD** becomes impatient.)*

BLUEBEARD. What the devil does the Dauphin mean by keeping us waiting like this? I don't know how you have the patience to stand there like a stone idol.

ARCHBISHOP. As Archbishop, I have learned to keep still and suffer fools patiently. *(Pause.)* Besides, it is the Dauphin's royal privilege to keep us waiting, is it not?

BLUEBEARD. Privilege be damned! Do you know how much money he owes me?

ARCHBISHOP. I take it he owes you everything you could afford to lend him. Which is also what he owes me.

BLUEBEARD. And what becomes of it all? He never has a suit of clothes that I would throw to a beggar. He dines on a chicken or a scrap of mutton. He borrows my last penny, and there is nothing to show for it.

> *(More discomfort and agitation. After a moment, the **PAGE** returns.)*

THE PAGE. His Majesty.

> *(They stand perfunctorily at court attention. The **DAUPHIN**, really **KING CHARLES** the Seventh since the death of his father, but as yet uncrowned, comes in through the curtains with a paper in his hands. He is a small man in both body and personality, and used to being pushed around by everyone. But at the moment, he is very excited about the letter he carries.)*

> *(**THE PAGE** stands aside, silent.)*

CHARLES. Oh, Archbishop, have you heard what Robert de Baudricourt is sending me from Vaucouleurs?

ARCHBISHOP. *(Contemptuously.)* I am not interested in the newest toys.

CHARLES. *(Indignantly.)* It isn't a toy. And I can get on very well without your interest.

ARCHBISHOP. Your Highness is taking offence very unnecessarily.

CHARLES. You're always ready with a lecture, aren't you?

BLUEBEARD. Enough grumbling. What have you got there?

CHARLES. What's it to you?

BLUEBEARD. It is my business to know what is passing between you and the garrison at Vaucouleurs.

> *(**BLUEBEARD** snatches the paper and begins reading it.)*

CHARLES. You all think you can treat me as you please because I owe you money, and because I am no good at fighting. But I have the blood royal in my veins!

ARCHBISHOP. Even that has been questioned, your Highness. One hardly recognizes in you the grandson of Charles the Wise.

CHARLES. No more about my grandfather! He was so wise that he used up the whole family supply of wisdom, and left me the poor fool I am, bullied and insulted by you.

ARCHBISHOP. Control yourself, sir. These outbursts of petulance are not seemly.

CHARLES. Another lecture! Thank you. What a pity it is that though you are an Archbishop, saints and angels don't come to see YOU.

ARCHBISHOP. What do you mean?

CHARLES. *(Pointing to* **BLUEBEARD**.*)* Ask that bully there. He's a fool but he's literate. I think.

BLUEBEARD. *(Shouting.)* Hold your tongue. Do you hear?

CHARLES. The whole castle can hear. You needn't shout. Why don't you go and shout at the English, and beat them for me?

BLUEBEARD. *(Raising his hand.)* You little –

CHARLES. *(Moving behind the* **ARCHBISHOP**.*)* Don't you raise your hand to me! It's high treason.

ARCHBISHOP. Come, come! We must keep some sort of order. *(To* **CHARLES**.*)* And you, sir: if you cannot rule your kingdom, at least try to rule yourself.

CHARLES. Yet another lecture!

BLUEBEARD. *(Handing over the paper to the* **ARCHBISHOP**.*)* Here: read.

ARCHBISHOP. *(Reading.)* I should have expected more common sense from de Baudricourt. He is sending some crackpot country lass here –

CHARLES. *(Interrupting.)* No. He is sending a saint: an angel. And she is coming to me: to me, the King, and not to you, Archbishop, holy as you are. She knows the blood royal even if you don't.

ARCHBISHOP. You cannot be allowed to see this crazy wench.

CHARLES. But I am the king; and I tell you I will. I am putting my foot down.

BLUEBEARD. Naughty! What would your wise grandfather say?

CHARLES. That just shows your ignorance, Bluebeard. My grandfather had a saint who used to float in the air when she was praying, and told him everything he wanted to know. My poor father had two saints! It is in our family; and I will have my saint, too.

ARCHBISHOP. This creature is not a saint. She is not even a respectable woman. She is dressed like a man, and rides round the country with soldiers. Such a person cannot be admitted to your Highness's court.

BLUEBEARD. *(Mischievously.)* We can easily find out whether she is an angel or not. Let us arrange when she comes that I shall pretend to be the Dauphin, and see whether she can find me out.

CHARLES. Yes: I agree to that. If she cannot find the blood royal I will have nothing to do with her.

ARCHBISHOP. It is for the Church to make saints: let de Baudricourt mind his own business. I say the girl shall not be admitted.

BLUEBEARD. But, Archbishop –

THE ARCHBISHOP. *(Sternly.)* I speak in the Church's name. *(To the* **DAUPHIN***.)* If you admit her, it will be in defiance of the Church.

CHARLES. *(Sulky.)* Well, if you make it an excommunication matter, I won't see her, of course. But you haven't read the end of the letter. De Baudricourt says she will save Orléans and beat the English.

BLUEBEARD. Rot!

CHARLES. Well, will <u>you</u> save Orléans for us, with all your bullying?

BLUEBEARD. *(Savagely.)* Do not throw that in my face again: do you hear? I have done more fighting than you ever did or ever will. But I cannot be everywhere.

ARCHBISHOP. Gentlemen, peace. Orléans is lost, in my opinion. It is only a matter of time before her citizens submit to the English. Better you should surrender the city, Sire, and seek refuge in Scotland or Aragon.

CHARLES. You would have me give up Orléans and her people, and flee like a coward?

ARCHBISHOP. You have Jack Dunois at the head of your troops in Orléans: the brave Dunois, the handsome Dunois, the wonderful invincible Dunois, the darling of all the ladies, the beautiful bastard. Is it likely that some country lass can do what he cannot do?

CHARLES. Why doesn't he raise the siege, then?

BLUEBEARD. The wind is against him.

CHARLES. How can the wind hurt him at Orléans? That's just an excuse.

BLUEBEARD. *(As though speaking to a child.)* Orléans is on the river Loire, and the English hold the bridge. Dunois must ship his men across the river and upstream. But he cannot, because there is a devil of a wind blowing the other way. What he needs is a miracle.

ARCHBISHOP. *(Who has now read the end of the letter.)* It is true that de Baudricourt seems extraordinarily impressed.

BLUEBEARD. De Baudricourt is a blazing ass; but he is a soldier; and if he thinks she can beat the English, all the rest of the army will think so too.

CHARLES. *(To the* **ARCHBISHOP**, *who is hesitating.)* Oh, let's hear her out! The bastard's men will give up Orléans in spite of him if somebody does not put some fire into them.

ARCHBISHOP. The Church must examine the girl before anything decisive is done about her. However, since his Highness desires it, let her attend the Court.

THE PAGE. I will tell her.

CHARLES. Come with me, Bluebeard; and let us arrange a test for her. You will pretend to be me.

>(**CHARLES** *exits through the curtains into the throne room.)*

BLUEBEARD. Pretend to be that thing? Holy Michael!

>(**BLUEBEARD** *follows* **CHARLES** *out.)*

THE PAGE. I wonder will she pick him out!

ARCHBISHOP. Of course she will.

THE PAGE. How will she know?

ARCHBISHOP. She will know what everybody in Chinon knows: that the Dauphin is the meanest-looking and worst-dressed figure in the Court, and that the man with the blue beard is Gilles de Rais.

THE PAGE. I never thought of that.

ARCHBISHOP. You are not so accustomed to miracles as I am. It is part of my profession.

THE PAGE. But that would not be a miracle at all.

ARCHBISHOP. *(Calmly.)* Why not?

PAGE. Well...then what is a miracle?

ARCHBISHOP. Miracles, my friend, are events which confirm or create faith.

THE PAGE. Even when they're frauds?

ARCHBISHOP. Frauds deceive. An event which creates faith does not deceive: therefore it is not a fraud, but a miracle. The Church must nourish the faith of men by poetry.

THE PAGE. Poetry! Begging your pardon, Archbishop, but I'd call it bullshit.

THE ARCHBISHOP. *(Indulgently.)* You would be wrong, my friend. Parables are not lies because they describe events that have never happened. Miracles are not frauds because they are often – not always – very simple contrivances by which the priest fortifies the faith of his flock. When this girl picks out the Dauphin among his courtiers, it will not be a miracle for me, because I shall

know how it has been done. But as for the others, if
they feel the thrill of the supernatural, and forget their
sinful clay in a sudden sense of the glory of God, it will
be a miracle and a blessed one. And you will find that
the girl herself will be more affected than anyone else.

THE PAGE. Well, come on, or we'll be late for the fun; and
I want to see it, miracle or no.

> *(They go out together through the curtains,
> which are presently withdrawn, revealing the
> full depth of the throne room with the Court
> assembled.)*

> *(*BLUEBEARD *is standing theatrically on the
> royal dais in front of the throne;* CHARLES
> *is hidden in the crowd, which includes the*
> BARONESS. *The* ARCHBISHOP *observes it all.)*

> *(*ST. CATHERINE *and* ST. MARGARET *are there.
> No one can see them but* JOAN. *They take
> up positions on either side of* CHARLES, *to
> indicate to* JOAN *who he is.)*

> *(*THE PAGE *enters.)*

Captain Robert de Baudricourt presents Joan the Maid
to his Majesty.

BLUEBEARD. *(Majestically.)* Let her approach the throne.

> *(*JOAN *enters, dressed as a soldier, with her
> hair bobbed or pinned up. She looks around
> eagerly for the Dauphin.* THE BARONESS
> *outright laughs at her.)*

THE BARONESS. *(To* BLUEBEARD.*)* *Mon dieu!* Her hair! The
poor unfortunate.

BLUEBEARD. Ssh – ssh! Baroness!

JOAN. *(Not embarrassed.)* I wear it like this because I'm a
soldier, and it gets in my way. Where is the Dauphin?

> *(A titter runs through the court as she walks
> to the dais.)*

BLUEBEARD. *(Condescendingly.)* You are in the presence of the Dauphin.

> *(**JOAN** looks at him skeptically. Dead silence, all watching her. Fun dawns in her face.)*

JOAN. You cannot fool me, Bluebeard! Where is the Dauphin?

> *(A roar of laughter breaks out as **BLUEBEARD**, with a gesture of surrender, jumps down from the dais. **JOAN**, grinning, searches along the row of courtiers, then drags out **CHARLES** by the arm.)*

(Releasing him and curtseying.) Gentle little Dauphin, I am sent to you to drive the English away from Orléans and from France, and to crown you king in the cathedral at Rheims, where all true kings of France are crowned.

CHARLES. *(Triumphantly.)* You see, all of you: she knew the blood royal. Who dare say now that I am not my father's son? *(To **JOAN**.)* But if you want me to be crowned at Rheims you must talk to the Archbishop, not to me.

> *(**CHARLES** points at the **ARCHBISHOP**.)*

JOAN. *(Overwhelmed.)* Oh, my lord!

> *(She falls on both knees before him.)*

My lord: I am only a poor country girl; and you are filled with the blessedness and glory of God Himself; but you will touch me with your hands, and give me your blessing, won't you?

BLUEBEARD. *(Whispering to the **BARONESS**).* The old fox blushes. Another miracle!

ARCHBISHOP. *(Touched, putting his hand on her head.)* Child: you are in love with religion.

JOAN. *(Startled, looking up at him.)* Is there any harm in it?

ARCHBISHOP. There is no harm in it, my child. But there is danger.

JOAN. *(Rising, happy.)* There is always danger, except in heaven. Oh, my lord, you have given me such strength, such courage. It must be a most wonderful thing to be Archbishop.

(The Court snickers at her earnest display.)

ARCHBISHOP. *(Reproachfully, to the Court.)* Your levity is rebuked by this maid's faith. I am, God help me, all unworthy; but your mirth is a deadly sin.

(Their faces fall. Silence.)

BLUEBEARD. My lord: we were laughing at her, not at you.

ARCHBISHOP. What? Not at my unworthiness but at her faith! Gilles de Rais: you will be hanged in your sin if you do not learn when to laugh and when to pray.

(There is more tittering.)

JOAN. *(Impatiently.)* Oh, my lord, please send all these silly folks away so that I may speak to the Dauphin alone.

ARCHBISHOP. Come, everyone. The Maid comes with God's blessing, and must be obeyed.

BLUEBEARD. *(With an empty smile.)* I can take a hint.

> *(The courtiers begin to leave. As the* **ARCHBISHOP** *passes* **JOAN**, *she falls on her knees, and kisses the hem of his robe. He shakes his head in instinctive demurral, gathers the robe from her, and goes out.)*

> *(***BLUEBEARD** *exits last.* **JOAN** *and* **CHARLES** *are alone.)*

JOAN. What is Bluebeard's job?

CHARLES. He pretends to command the army. And he bullies me. They all bully me.

JOAN. You're afraid?

CHARLES. Yes: I am afraid. It's all very well for these big men with their muscles and their shouting and their bad tempers. They like fighting. But I am quiet and sensible. I don't want to kill people: I only want to be left alone to enjoy myself.

JOAN. We are all like that to begin with! Do you think I've come to you because I like fighting and killing people? I'm just as unlikely as you are.

CHARLES. So why do they follow you, if you're no real soldier?

JOAN. Because I am willing to put my fear aside and go first. And I shall put courage into you, too.

CHARLES. *(Annoyed.)* But I don't want to have courage put into me. I want to sleep in a comfortable bed, and not live in continual terror of being killed or wounded. Put courage into the others, but let me alone. I never asked to be a king!

JOAN. It's no use, Charlie: you must face what God puts on you. What else are you fit for? Come! Let me see you sitting on the throne. I have looked forward to that.

CHARLES. What is the good of sitting on the throne when the other fellows give all the orders? However!

(He sits enthroned, petulant.)

Here is the king for you! Look your fill at the poor devil.

JOAN. You're not king yet – still just the Dauphin. Listen to me: I know the people, the real people that make your bread for you. And I tell you they count no man king of France until he is consecrated and crowned in Rheims Cathedral. And you need new clothes, Charlie. Why does not the Queen look after you properly?

CHARLES. We're too poor. She wants all the money we can spare to put on her own back. Besides, I don't care what I wear myself.

JOAN. Hmm. A bit of modesty. There is some good in you, Charlie, but it is not yet a king's good.

CHARLES. We shall see. I am not such a fool as I look. I can tell you that one good treaty is worth ten good fights. If we can only have a treaty, we will surely best the English. They're better at fighting than at thinking.

JOAN. But if the English win the fight, it is they that will make the treaty, and then God help poor France!

> (**CHARLES** *is quiet, not conceding her valid point.)*

You must fight, Charlie, whether you want to or not. You have no more choice than I have. I will go first to hearten you. We must take our courage in both hands: aye, and pray for it with both hands, too.

CHARLES. *(Descending from his throne.)* Oh do stop talking about God and praying. I can't bear people who are always praying. Isn't it bad enough to have to do it at the proper times?

JOAN. *(Pitying him.)* You poor child, you've never prayed in your life. I must teach you from the beginning.

CHARLES. I am not a child: I am a grown man and a father, and I will not be taught any more. I want to be just what I am. Why can't you mind your own business, and let me mind mine?

JOAN. *(Contemptuous.)* What is my business? Helping mother at home. What is yours? Petting lapdogs and sucking sugar-sticks. I call that muck. I have a message for you from God; and you must listen to it, though your heart breaks with the terror of it. You must shepherd God's flock in France – this is the mantle you were born to wear. Put it on and rise!

CHARLES. I don't want a message – but can you tell me any secrets? Can you do any cures? Can you turn lead into gold, or anything of that sort?

JOAN. I can turn you into a king. And that is a miracle that will take some doing, it seems.

CHARLES. But, if you could just give me a sign –

JOAN. In God's name, I did not come here to give signs! Take me to Orléans, and I will show you what I am sent for. *(Short pause.)* I come from God to tell you to kneel in the cathedral and solemnly give your kingdom to Him for ever and ever, and become the greatest king in the world as His soldier and His servant. The very clay of France will become holy: her soldiers will be the soldiers of God. The English will fall on their knees and beg you let them return to their lawful homes.

CHARLES. And then what?

JOAN. Peace. Will you be a poor little Judas, and betray me and Him that sent me?

CHARLES. *(Tempted at last.)* Oh, if I only dare!

JOAN. I shall dare, dare, and dare again, in God's name! Give your kingdom to God, and you will never again be defeated, or bullied, or cast aside, in all your long life. *(Short pause.)* Go forward bravely. Fear nothing. If you will go forward like a man, you shall have your whole kingdom.

CHARLES. *(Excited.)* I'll risk it. I give my kingdom to God. I place it in your hands.

JOAN. Then receive it back from him as his faithful steward. You cannot now be defeated by any force on earth.

> (**CHARLES** *once again approaches the dais, more confident than we have yet seen him, and calls out.)*

CHARLES. With God as my witness, I give command of my army to The Maid. The Maid is to do as she likes with it.

JOAN. To Orléans!

CHARLES. For God and His Maid! To Orléans!

> (**JOAN**, *radiant, falls on her knees in thanksgiving to God.)*

Interlude One – Joan's Sword

(A small country chapel: the Church of Sainte-Catherine-de-Fierbois. March 1429.)

*(**JOAN** marches in with purpose, trailed by a confused **ABBESS**, who lives and works at the chapel.)*

ABBESS. I tell you there is nothing buried behind our altar!

JOAN. My voices said I would find it here.

ABBESS. My dear, I scrub that floor on my hands and knees every day. I have seen nothing like what you describe.

JOAN. *(Turning to her.)* This is the chapel of Sainte-Catherine-de-Fierbois? Where prisoners of war make pilgrimage to give thanks for deliverance from captivity?

ABBESS. Yes, but they leave broken chains and cracked armor. No one would leave behind his sword! *(Kindly.)* Surely, the Dauphin can give you a sword.

JOAN. I have been given two – but neither is my true sword. My true sword was buried under this altar by the grandfather of Charlemagne – to wait for the next person whom God would choose to deliver France. It must be here.

ABBESS. *(Flustered)*. Perhaps...perhaps I should just quickly inform the bishop...

*(The **ABBESS** exits, hurriedly. **ST. CATHERINE** and **ST. MARGARET** appear.)*

JOAN. Why is it so hard for her to believe in me? A bride of Christ.

ST. CATHERINE. Your relationship with Christ is hard for people to comprehend, Jehanne. Even other true believers. Pray for her, and do not let her doubt deter you.

*(**JOAN** wastes not a moment. She approaches the altar, makes the sign of the cross, and digs a little behind it. She soon finds the sword*

that was promised to her. It is rusty and dirty.)

JOAN. Exactly as you described. Another promise kept.

ST. MARGARET. The Sword of Sainte Catherine has seen many great battles. Does it suit you?

(**JOAN** *is quiet for a long moment.)*

JOAN. The others I held were new. This sword has shed blood.

ST. CATHERINE. But it never will again.

JOAN. *(Surprised.)* What?

ST. CATHERINE. Your sword is to remain pristine, beloved Jehanne.

JOAN. But –

ST. CATHERINE. *(Interrupting.)* You are tasked with ending the bloodshed in France, not adding to it. You must never raise this sword to kill a child of God. Even the English are children of God.

JOAN. But I will need to protect myself.

ST. MARGARET. You have our protection.

JOAN. But...but...am I not a warrior?

ST. MARGARET. You are more than that. You are the very spirit of victory.

JOAN. *(Sputtering.)* The...the villages...the bodies... You said I would lead an army!

ST. CATHERINE. You will, child of God.

JOAN. The *goddams* drove us from our village with only what we could carry. We returned to a wasteland. The crops all burned, the houses pillaged, the church destroyed. The CHURCH! Even the insects were gone. It took us a year to rebuild. Every day fearing they would come back.

ST. MARGARET. *(A warning.)* Banish these dark thoughts.

JOAN. And on the way to Chinon, the men and I passed through that village –

ST. CATHERINE. *(Interrupting gently.)* We were with you. We are always with you.

JOAN. *(Continuing.)* The *goddams* had killed everyone. Women with their skirts pulled up, lying violated in pools of their own blood. Farmer's bodies severed from their heads, still holding their useless pitchforks. They killed the babies. They killed the horses and dogs! Vultures picked at the bodies until we ran them off. Those poor souls – murdered in terror, unshriven, unprepared.

ST. MARGARET. *(Not dismissively.)* That is war, Jehanne.

JOAN. The men would not let me bury them! They said the dead would have to get their help from God. As soon as we rode on, the vultures circled back. I dream of those people, I see their dead faces when I close my eyes. And the ONLY reason I was able to leave them that day, was because YOU assured me that God would send an all-powerful army to avenge them. And I would lead that army. You promised.

ST. MARGARET. We will keep that promise. As we have all the others.

JOAN. But am I not allowed to avenge my people by my own hand?! Am I not allowed to make my sword sing the way all soldiers do, to take blood for blood in remembrance of those villagers, in remembrance of my own family's suffering?

ST. CATHERINE. The *goddams* are not your enemy.

JOAN. Oh yes they are. They are monsters.

ST. CATHERINE. WAR is your enemy, Jehanne. Do you really believe that French soldiers would not leave English villages in the same state?

JOAN. French soldiers would never plunder. We have God's backing.

ST. MARGARET. War turns the noblest purpose into justification for horrors. You cannot let the darkness of it touch your soul. Even now, your rage threatens to drive you off course.

JOAN. *(Furious.)* So I will not be a warrior at all?! And this sword is just a costume piece. To inspire others to follow me where I cannot actually go.

ST. CATHERINE. Do not hate, Jehanne.

JOAN. Why not? They hate us. I cannot pretend I have not seen what I have seen.

ST. MARGARET. Hatred can only lead you away from God. The men who destroyed that village are fearful and lost. They have forgotten God's love for them, but God has not forgotten. God does not love them less for what they have done – how can you hate them? Is your judgement superior to His?

ST. CATHERINE. You must forgive your enemies to do the will of God. And once you have truly forgiven them, you will find that you have no enemies. Your mind will be clear. You cannot bring peace to France without also bringing peace to England.

JOAN. So these men may do as they wish, but I must be a good girl and keep my hands clean?

ST. CATHERINE. Yes. In so doing, you will lift the whole world up to meet you.

> (**JOAN** *is calmer now. She is trying to forgive; she knows they are right. She knocks the dirt and rust from her sword, and it falls off easily. The sword gleams.*)

JOAN. (*Holding the sword.*) So what is this, then?

ST. CATHERINE. A symbol – that the soul of France is in good hands.

> (**ST. CATHERINE** *and* **ST. MARGARET** *fade. The* **ABBESS** *returns, with the* **BISHOP**. *They see the gleaming sword in* **JOAN**'s *hand, and both fall to their knees immediately.*)

ABBESS. God be praised. She has come to deliver us.

> (*Lights dim on the chapel.*)

Scene Three

(Orléans, 29 April, 1429.)

*(**JEAN DE DUNOIS**, cousin of the Dauphin and commander of the troops at Orléans, is pacing up and down the south bank of the Loire, commanding a long view of the river in both directions. He is a good-natured man and a capable commander.)*

*(His **LIEUTENANT** stands nearby. Both men watch the river. **DUNOIS** sticks his arm up in the air and wiggles his fingers a bit.)*

DUNOIS. *(Wearily.)* Change, curse you, change, English harlot of a wind, change. West, west, I tell you. *(Pause.)* False wind from over the water, will you never blow again?

LIEUTENANT. *(Excited.)* Look! There! There she goes!

DUNOIS. *(Eagerly.)* Where? Who? The Maid?

LIEUTENANT. *(Embarrassed.)* No, a...a kingfisher. Like blue lightning. She went into that bush. Sorry, sir.

> *(They follow the flight till the bird takes cover. **JOAN** enters in splendid white armor. She rushes in in a blazing hurry.)*

(Turning around and seeing her.) Halt! Who goes there?

JOAN. *(Ignoring this.)* Are you the Bastard of Orléans?

DUNOIS. Are you Joan the Maid?

JOAN. Surely.

DUNOIS. Where are your troops?

JOAN. Miles behind. They have cheated me. They have brought me to the wrong side of the river.

DUNOIS. I told them to.

JOAN. Why did you do that? The English are on the other side!

DUNOIS. Well, actually, the English are on both sides.

JOAN. But Orléans is on the other side! We must fight the English there. How can we cross the river?

DUNOIS. *(Grimly.)* There is a bridge.

JOAN. In God's name, then, let us cross the bridge, and fall on them.

DUNOIS. It seems simple; but it cannot be done.

JOAN. Who says so?

DUNOIS. I say so; and older and wiser heads than mine are of the same opinion.

JOAN. Then your older and wiser heads are fatheads: they have made a fool of you, and now they want to make a fool of me too! Do you not know that I bring you better help than ever came to any general or any town?

DUNOIS. *(Smiling.)* Your own?

JOAN. No: the help and counsel of the King of Heaven. Act, and God will act. Which way to the bridge?

DUNOIS. You are impatient, Maid.

JOAN. Is this a time for patience? Our enemy is at our gates, and here we stand doing nothing. Oh, why are you not fighting? Listen to me: I will deliver you from fear. I –

DUNOIS. *(Interrupting, laughing.)* If you deliver me from fear I will be a good knight for a story book, but a very bad commander of the army. Come! Let me begin to make a soldier of you.

(He takes her to the water's edge.)

Do you see those two forts at this end of the bridge? The English hold them, and they are heavily fortified. We stand to lose too many men if we try to take them.

JOAN. They cannot hold those forts against God. I will take those forts.

DUNOIS. Not a man will follow you.

JOAN. I will not look back to see whether anyone is following me.

DUNOIS. *(Recognizing her mettle.)* Good. You have the makings of a soldier. You are in love with fighting.

JOAN. *(Gravely.)* No. Not I. Never.

DUNOIS. But you have thrown yourself into a war, and war is all about fighting.

JOAN. Perhaps the first day of war is for fighting. All the days after are for peace.

DUNOIS. I, God forgive me, am a little in love with war myself. I am like a man with two wives. Do you want to be like a woman with two husbands?

JOAN. *(Matter-of-fact.)* I will never take a husband; my voices have sworn it. I am a soldier: I do not care for the things women care for. They dream of lovers, and of safety. I dream of leading a charge, and of placing the big guns. I will be first up the ladder when we reach the fort, Bastard. I dare you to follow me.

DUNOIS. Joan, you must know that I welcome you as a saint, not as a soldier. I have daredevils enough at my call, as if they could help me.

JOAN. I am not a daredevil: I am a servant of God. My sword is sacred and I may not strike a killing blow with it.

DUNOIS. Can you at least defend yourself?

JOAN. *(Plainly.)* Not well. But God defends me.

DUNOIS. Would God mind if I taught you some blocking maneuvers?

JOAN. *(Resuming her haste.)* I will lead, Bastard, and your men will follow. That is all I can do. But I must do it: you shall not stop me.

DUNOIS. You are no good to me as a saint or a symbol or anything else, if the enemy cuts your head off in the first five minutes. *(Gentler.)* Let me teach you.

> (**JOAN** *sighs, then nods assent.*)

> (*There is a short moment of fight choreography in which the* **LIEUTENANT** *demonstrates to* **JOAN** *a very basic block. She learns quickly, and she and the* **LIEUTENANT** *repeat the move throughout the next bit of dialogue. She is slow, but consistent and adept.*)

You learn quickly, soldier.

JOAN. I always have.

DUNOIS. Now. You see our problem is this: our men cannot take those forts by a sally across the bridge. They must come by water, and take the English from the rear on this side.

JOAN. Then make rafts and put big guns on them, and let your men cross to us.

DUNOIS. The rafts are ready; and the men are embarked. But they must wait for God.

JOAN. What do you mean? God is waiting for them!

(The swordplay stops.)

DUNOIS. Let Him send us a wind then. My boats are downstream: they cannot come up against both wind and current. Come: let me take you to the church.

JOAN. No. I love the church, but the English will not yield to prayers: they understand nothing but hard knocks and slashes. I will not go to church until we have beaten them.

DUNOIS. You must come along to church to pray for a West Wind. I have prayed, but my prayers are not answered. Yours may be.

JOAN. Oh, yes! I will pray to Saint Catherine and Saint Margaret. They will ask God to send us a West Wind.

*(**JOAN** drops to her knees.)*

DUNOIS. What? Here?

THE PAGE. *(Sneezes violently.)* At-cha!!!

JOAN. God bless you, Lieutenant. Kneel, Bastard. Hope in God. If you have good hope and faith in him, you shall be delivered from your enemies.

> *(**DUNOIS** looks skeptical, but he takes a knee as well. The **LIEUTENANT** shivers. Then wiggles his fingers in the air.)*

LIEUTENANT. Seigneur! Seigneur! Mademoiselle!

JOAN. We're praying, sir.

DUNOIS. What is it? The bird again?

LIEUTENANT. No: the wind, the wind, the wind! That is what made me sneeze.

DUNOIS. *(Feeling it on his face.)* The wind has changed.

> *(Crossing himself.)*

God has spoken.

> *(Handing his baton to* **JOAN**.*)*

You command the king's army. I am your soldier.

LIEUTENANT. *(Looking down the river.)* The boats have put off. They are ripping upstream like lightening!

DUNOIS. *(Rising.)* Now for the forts! You dared me to follow. Dare you lead?

JOAN. *(Flinging her arms round* **DUNOIS**, *kissing him on both cheeks.)* Dunois, dear comrade in arms: set my foot on the ladder, and say "Up, Joan."

DUNOIS. *(Dragging her out.)* Never mind the celebration: make for the flash of battle!

JOAN. *(In a blaze of courage.)* I will raise such a war-cry against them as shall be remembered forever!

DUNOIS. *(Dragging her along with him.)* For God and Saint Denis!

JOAN. For Saint Margaret and Saint Catherine and Saint Michael!

> *(All three run out, mad with excitement.)*

> *(Lights dim on the river bank.)*

Scene Four

(A small room in a grand English *castle.)*

(An English chaplain with a narrow mind and a loose tongue, **STOGUMBER**, *sits on a stool at a table, furiously writing. At the other side of the table an imposing English noblewoman, the* **COUNTESS LADY WARWICK**, *is turning over the leaves of an illuminated Book of Hours.)*

LADY WARWICK. Now this is what I call workmanship. There is nothing on earth more exquisite than a bonny book, with well-placed columns of rich black writing in beautiful borders, and illuminated pictures cunningly inset. But nowadays, instead of looking at books, people read them. It's such a shame.

STOGUMBER. I must say, my lady, you take your husband's defeat very coolly. Very coolly indeed.

LADY WARWICK. That happens, you know. It is only in history books and ballads that the enemy is always defeated.

STOGUMBER. But we English are being defeated over and over again. First, Orléans –

LADY WARWICK. *(Pooh-poohing.)* Oh, Orléans! A clear case of witchcraft and sorcery.

STOGUMBER. And we are still being defeated! Jargeau, Meung, Beaugency, and now we have been butchered at Patay.

(Throwing down his pen, almost in tears.)

By God, if this goes on any longer I will fling my cassock to the devil, take arms myself, and strangle her with my own hands. I cannot stand by and see us beaten by a French bastard and a village witch from lousy Champagne.

By God, if this goes on any longer, I will fling my cassock to the devil, take arms myself, and strangle the accursed witch with my own hands!

LADY WARWICK. *(Laughing at him.)* So you shall, chaplain, so you shall, if we can do nothing better. But not yet, not quite yet. We shall burn the witch and beat the bastard all in good time. Indeed, I am waiting at present for the Bishop of Beauvais, to arrange the burning with him.

(**STOGUMBER** *calms himself, and sulks.*)

STOGUMBER. A French bishop? Why would he want to burn the "Maid of Orléans"? The peasants love her.

LADY WARWICK. Yes, the <u>peasants</u> do. The clergy are another matter. This bishop has been turned out of his diocese by her cult. My husband shall offer a king's ransom for her capture.

STOGUMBER. A king's ransom! For that slut?

LADY WARWICK. One has to leave a margin. Some of Charles's people will sell her to the Burgundians; the Burgundians will sell her to us; and there will probably be three or four middlemen who will want their little commissions. It all adds up.

(**BISHOP CAUCHON** *enters.*)

And here he is: the Right Reverend Bishop of Beauvais: Monseigneur Cauchon. My dear Bishop, how good of you to come! Allow me to introduce myself: Isabel le Despenser, Countess of Worcester and Warwick, at your service.

CAUCHON. Your ladyship's fame is well known to me. As is your honorable husband's.

LADY WARWICK. You are too kind.

CAUCHON. The Earl is your second husband, is he not?

LADY WARWICK. He is. My first, the Earl of Worchester, was killed at the Siege of Meaux.

CAUCHON. You have made a very advantageous second arrangement.

LADY WARWICK. I excel at advantageous arrangements. Which, I believe, is what has brought you here today.

(She smiles at him, confidently.)

This reverend cleric is Master John de Stogumber.

STOGUMBER. *(Grandly.)* John Bowyer Spenser Neville de Stogumber, at your service, my lord: Bachelor of Theology, and Keeper of the Private Seal to His Eminence the Cardinal of Winchester.

LADY WARWICK. *(To* **CAUCHON**.*)* Our king's uncle.

CAUCHON. Monsieur John de Stogumber: I am always the very good friend of His Eminence.

> *(***CAUCHON*** extends his hand to the Chaplain who kisses his ring.)*

LADY WARWICK. Do me the honor to be seated.

> *(***LADY WARWICK*** gives* **CAUCHON** *the place of honor at the head of the table, then gets down to business.)*

Well, my Lord Bishop, you find us in one of our unlucky moments. Charles is to be crowned at Rheims, practically <u>by</u> the young woman from Lorraine; we cannot prevent it. I suppose it will make a great difference to Charles's position.

CAUCHON. Undoubtedly. It is a masterstroke of The Maid's.

STOGUMBER. *(Agitated.)* We were not fairly beaten, my lord. No Englishman is ever fairly beaten.

> *(***CAUCHON*** raises his eyebrow, then quickly composes his face.)*

LADY WARWICK. Our friend here takes the view that the young woman is a sorceress. It would, I presume, be the duty of your reverend lordship to denounce her to the Inquisition and have her burnt for that offence.

CAUCHON. If she were captured in my diocese: yes. But we shall have to consider not merely our own opinions here, but the prejudices of a French court.

LADY WARWICK. *(Correcting.)* A Catholic court, my lord.

CAUCHON. Catholic courts are composed of mortal men, like other courts. And if the men are Frenchmen, I am afraid the bare fact that an English army has been defeated by a French one will not convince them that there is any sorcery in the matter.

STOGUMBER. *(Chafing.)* My lord: at Orléans this woman had her throat pierced by an English arrow. It was a death wound; yet she fought all day, and walked alone to the wall of our fort with a white banner in her hand; and our men were paralyzed, and could neither shoot nor strike whilst the French fell on them and drove them on to the bridge, which immediately burst into flames and crumbled under them. They were drowned in heaps. Was this your bastard's generalship, or witchcraft?

CAUCHON. I do not say that there were no supernatural powers on her side. But the names on that white banner were not the names of Satan and Beelzebub, but the blessed names of our Lord and His holy mother.

LADY WARWICK. Well, what are we to infer from all this, my lord? Has The Maid converted you?

CAUCHON. If she had, my lady, I would not be here with you now.

(A tense silence between them.)

CAUCHON. Now, Lady Warwick, if the devil is making use of this girl – and I believe he is –

LADY WARWICK. *(Interrupting, reassured.)* Ah! You hear, Messire John? I knew your lordship would not fail us. Pardon my interruption. Proceed.

CAUCHON. If it be so, the devil has longer views than you give him credit for.

LADY WARWICK. Indeed? In what way?

CAUCHON. If the devil wanted to damn a country girl, do you think so easy a task would cost him half a dozen battles? No, my lady. The Prince of Darkness does not condescend to such cheap drudgery. When he strikes, he strikes at the Catholic Church, whose realm is the whole spiritual world. When he damns, he damns the souls of the entire human race.

STOGUMBER. I told you she was a witch.

CAUCHON. She is not a witch. She is a <u>heretic</u>.

STOGUMBER. What difference does that make?

CAUCHON. *(Fiercely.)* You, a priest, ask me that! The woman's "miracles" would not impose on a rabbit: she does not claim them as miracles herself. What do her victories prove but that she has a better head on her shoulders than any of you?

LADY WARWICK. My lord: I wipe the slate as far as the witchcraft goes. None the less, we must burn the woman.

CAUCHON. I cannot burn her. The Church cannot take life. And my first duty is to seek this girl's salvation.

LADY WARWICK. No doubt. *(Short pause.)* But you do burn people occasionally.

CAUCHON. No. When The Church cuts off an obstinate heretic as a dead branch from the tree of life, the heretic is handed over to the secular arm. The Church has no part in what the secular arm may see fit to do.

LADY WARWICK. Precisely. My husband and I shall be the secular arm in this case. Well, my lord, hand over your dead branch; and we will see that the fire is ready for it. If you will answer for The Church's part, we will answer for the secular part.

CAUCHON. *(With smoldering anger.)* You great lords are too prone to treat The Church as a mere political convenience.

WARWICK. Not in England, I assure you.

CAUCHON. Do not smile at me as if I were repeating meaningless words. She must have a fair trial. The soul of this village girl is of equal value with yours or your husband's or your king's before the throne of God.

STOGUMBER. *(Rising in a fury.)* You are a traitor.

CAUCHON. You lie, priest. *And* if you dare do what this woman has done – set your country above the Holy Catholic Church – you shall go to the fire with her.

STOGUMBER. My lord: I – I went too far.

(He sits down in submission.)

LADY WARWICK. I must apologize on my own account if I have seemed to take the burning of this poor girl too lightly. When one has seen whole countrysides burnt over and over again...one has to grow a very thick skin. May I venture to assume that your lordship also, having to see so many heretics burned from time to time, is compelled to take – shall I say – a professional view of what would otherwise be a very horrible incident?

CAUCHON. Yes, it is a painful duty, even, as you say, a horrible one. But I am not thinking of this girl's body, which will suffer for a few moments only, but of her soul, which may suffer to all eternity.

LADY WARWICK. Just so; God grant that her soul may be saved! But the practical problem would seem to be how to save her soul <u>without</u> saving her body. We must face it, my lord: if this cult of The Maid goes on, we are all lost.

STOGUMBER. *(Carefully.)* May I speak, my lady?

LADY WARWICK. Really, I had rather you did not.

STOGUMBER. It is only this. The Maid is deceitfully devout. Her prayers and confessions are endless. How can she be accused of heresy when she neglects no observance of a faithful daughter of The Church?

CAUCHON. *(Flaming up.)* A faithful daughter of The Church! The Pope himself at his proudest dare not presume as this woman presumes. She acts as if she herself were The Church. She brings the message of God to Charles, and The Church must stand aside. She will crown him in the cathedral of Rheims: she, not The Church! She sends letters to the king of England giving him God's command through her. Has she ever in all her utterances said one word of The Church? Never.

It is always God and herself. And she is spreading this heresy everywhere! What will it be when every girl thinks herself a Joan?

LADY WARWICK. *(Her patience is wearing out.)* My Lord Bishop, I am not arguing with you. But pray get The Church out of your head for a moment; and remember that there are temporal institutions in the world as well as spiritual ones. I and my peers represent the feudal aristocracy as you represent The Church. Do you not see how this girl strikes at us? Her idea is that the kings should give their realms to God, and then reign as God's bailiffs.

CAUCHON. *(Not interested.)* It is an abstract idea: a mere form of words.

LADY WARWICK. No. It is a cunning device to supersede the aristocracy. Instead of the king being merely the first among his peers, he becomes their master. That we cannot suffer: we call no man master.

CAUCHON. Need you fear that? You are the makers of kings after all. They reign according to your pleasure.

LADY WARWICK. Yes, as long as the people follow their feudal lords, and know the king only as a traveling show. If the people's hearts were turned to the king, he could break us across his knee one by one.

CAUCHON. But where would the king find counsellors to plan and carry out such a policy for him?

LADY WARWICK. *(Grimly.)* Perhaps in the Church, my lord.

> **(CAUCHON,** *with a sour smile, shrugs his shoulders, and does not contradict her.)*

CAUCHON. *(Conciliatory.)* My lady: we shall not defeat The Maid if we strive against one another. I see now that what is in your mind is not that this girl has never once mentioned The Church, and thinks only of God and herself – but that she has never once mentioned the aristocracy, and thinks only of the king and herself.

LADY WARWICK. Quite so. These two ideas of hers are the same idea at the bottom. It goes deep, my lord. I should call it Protestantism if I had to find a name for it.

CAUCHON. You understand it wonderfully well, my lady.

STOGUMBER. That is not to be endured! Let her perish! Let her burn! Let her not infect the whole flock. It is expedient that one woman die for the people.

LADY WARWICK. My lord: we seem to be agreed.

CAUCHON. *(Protesting.)* I will not imperil my soul. I will uphold the justice of the Church. I will strive to the utmost for this woman's salvation.

LADY WARWICK. I am sorry for the poor girl. I hate these severities. I will spare her if I can.

STOGUMBER. *(Implacably.)* I would burn her with my own hands.

CAUCHON. *(Blessing the* **LADY**.*) Sancta simplicitas*[*].

    (Lights dim.)

---

[*] This Latin phrase means "holy innocence," and is often used ironically in reference to another's naïveté.

Coronation

(A short scene takes place without words, in which we see **JOAN** *place the crown on* **CHARLES**'s *head in Rheims Cathedral. Music plays*, the people rejoice. The once-Dauphin is now rightful King of all France.)*

(All onstage bend the knee in reverence to **CHARLES**. **CHARLES** *gloats.* **DUNOIS** *is pleased, but reserved.* **JOAN** *is triumphant.)*

JOAN. Gentle king, now is fulfilled the good pleasure of God.

(But the **ARCHBISHOP** *looks sour. Dark clouds are gathering. Lights dim on the coronation.)*

Intermission

---

* A license to produce *Saint Joan* does not include a performance license for any third-party or copyrighted music. Licensees should create an original composition or use music in the public domain. For further information, please see Music Use Note on page 3.

Scene Five

(July 1429.)

(A small courtyard of the cathedral at Rheims, near the doors. The organ is playing the people out of the nave after the coronation. **JOAN** is practicing with her sword; all the pomp and circumstance has made her restless and itchy. She is beautifully dressed, but still in male attire. **DUNOIS**, also splendidly arrayed, enters.)*

DUNOIS. Come, Joan! It is all over: the cathedral is empty; and the streets are full. They are calling for The Maid.

JOAN. No. Let the king have all the glory.

DUNOIS. He only spoils the show, poor devil. No, Joan: you have crowned him; and you must go through with it.

*(**JOAN** shakes her head adamantly and engages him in sparring. He joins in happily. They spar while they talk throughout the scene until **CHARLES** enters.)*

*(We see how skilled **JOAN** has become with her sword. It is an extension of her arm now, and she counters **DUNOIS** easily.)*

Come, come! It will be over in a couple of hours. It's better than the bridge at Orléans, eh?

JOAN. Oh, dear Dunois, how I wish it were the bridge at Orléans again! We lived at that bridge.

DUNOIS. Yes, faith, and died too: some of us. *(Teasing.)* You must learn to be restrained in your warring, just as you are in your food and drink, my little saint.

JOAN. You are the pick of the basket here, Jack: the only friend I have among all these nobles.

DUNOIS. And you need a friend, poor innocent child of God.

JOAN. Why do all these courtiers and knights and churchmen hate me? What have I done to them? I have brought them luck and victory: I have made sure they knew when they were doing all sorts of stupid things: I have crowned Charles and made him a real king; and all the honors he is handing out have gone to <u>them</u>. Then why do they not love me?

DUNOIS. *(Good naturedly.)* You sweet simpleton! Do you expect stupid people to love you for revealing their stupidity? Do blundering old military generals love the successful young captains who show them up? Do archbishops enjoy being played off their own altars, even by saints? Why, I'd be jealous of you myself if I were ambitious enough.

JOAN. They needn't worry about my ambitions. I have asked nothing for myself. *(Shrugging.)* Perhaps I will go back to the farm when I have taken Paris.

DUNOIS. I am not so sure that they will let you take Paris.

(She stops sparring.)

JOAN. *(Startled.)* What!

DUNOIS. I should have taken it myself before this if they had all been in agreement. Some of them would rather Paris took you, I think. So take care.

JOAN. Jack: the world is too wicked for me. If the *goddams* do not make an end of me, the French will. If not for my voices I should lose all heart. That is why I had to steal away to pray here alone after the coronation. Here in this corner, where the bells come down from heaven, and the echoes linger – my voices are in them.

(The cathedral clock chimes.)

*(***DUNOIS*** re-engages her with his sword, and **JOAN** joins in.)*

DUNOIS. *(Kindly, but not sympathetically.)* You make me uneasy when you talk about your voices: I should think you were a bit cracked if I hadn't noticed that you give me very sensible reasons for what you do.

JOAN. *(Crossly.)* The voices come first, and I find the reasons for you after.

DUNOIS. Are you angry, Joan?

JOAN. Yes. No: not with you. I am never angry with you.

*(***DUNOIS*** looks at her sideways for a moment. His ego cannot help but interpret this as flirtation.)*

DUNOIS. You are a bit of a woman after all.

JOAN. No: not a bit. I am a soldier and nothing else.

*(***KING CHARLES*** enters with ***BLUEBEARD*** from the vestry, where he has been disrobing. **JOAN** shrinks away.)*

DUNOIS. Well, your Majesty is an anointed king at last. How do you like it?

CHARLES. I would not go through it again to be emperor of the sun and moon. The weight of those robes! I thought I would drop when she loaded that crown onto me. And the famous holy oil they talked so much about was rancid: phew! The Archbishop must be nearly dead: his robes must have weighed a ton.

DUNOIS. *(Drily.)* Your majesty should wear armor oftener. That would accustom you to heavy dressing.

CHARLES. Yes: the old jibe! Well, I'm not going to wear armor; fighting is not my job. Where is The Maid?

JOAN. *(Coming forward and falling on her knee.)* Sire: I have made you king. My work is nearly done. I will soon be going back to my father's farm.

CHARLES. *(Surprised and relieved.)* Oh! Well, that will be very nice.

(**JOAN** *rises, deeply discouraged.*)

A healthy life, you know.

DUNOIS. But a dull one.

BLUEBEARD. You will find the petticoats tripping you up after leaving them off for so long. And you will miss the fighting. It's a bad habit, but a grand one, and the hardest of all to break.

CHARLES. *(Anxiously.)* Still, we don't want you to stay if you would really rather go home.

JOAN. *(Bitterly.)* I know well that none of you will be sorry to see me go.

BLUEBEARD. Well, I shall be able to swear when I want to. I look forward to that.

JOAN. Jack: do you think you will be able to drive them out?

DUNOIS. *(With quiet conviction.)* Yes: I shall drive them out. They have no roots here. I have beaten them before; and I shall beat them again.

JOAN. *(Suddenly.)* But before I go home, let us take Paris!

CHARLES. *(Terrified.)* Oh no, no. We shall lose everything we have gained. Oh, don't let us have any more fighting. We can make a very good treaty with the Duke of Burgundy.

JOAN. Treaty!

CHARLES. Well, why not, now that I am crowned and anointed?

(*The* **ARCHBISHOP** *comes from the vestry and joins the group.*)

Archbishop: The Maid wants to start fighting again.

ARCHBISHOP. Are we at peace, then?

CHARLES. Let us be content with what we have done! Let us make a treaty. Our luck is too good to last; and now is our chance to stop before it turns.

JOAN. Luck! God has fought for us, and you call it luck! And you would stop while there are still Englishmen on this holy earth of dear France!

ARCHBISHOP. *(Sternly.)* Maid: the king addressed himself to me, not to you. You forget yourself. You very often forget yourself.

JOAN. *(Unabashed, and roughly.)* Then speak, you, and tell him that it is not God's will that he should take his hand from the plough.

ARCHBISHOP. When you first came you respected me, and would not have dared to speak as you are now speaking. You came clothed with the virtue of humility; and because God blessed your enterprises accordingly, you have stained yourself with the sin of pride.

CHARLES. Yes: she thinks she knows better than everyone else.

JOAN. *(Distressed, but naïvely incapable of seeing the effect she is producing.)* But I do know better than any of you seem to. And I am not proud: I never speak unless I know I am right.

BLUEBEARD.	CHARLES.
Ha!	Just so.

ARCHBISHOP. How do you know you are right?

JOAN. I always know. My voices –

CHARLES. *(Interrupting.)* Oh, your voices, your voices. Why don't the voices come to me? I am king, not you!

JOAN. They do come to you; but you do not listen for them. If you prayed from your heart, you would hear the voices as well as I do.

(Turning brusquely from him.)

I tell you we must make a dash at Compiègne and relieve it as we relieved Orléans. Then Paris will open its gates; or if not, we will break through them. What is your crown worth without your capital?

BLUEBEARD. That is what I say too. We shall go through them like a red hot shot through a pound of butter. What do you say, Bastard?

DUNOIS. Pluck and impetuosity are good servants in war, but bad masters. We never know when we are beaten: that is our great fault.

JOAN. You never know when you are victorious: that is a worse fault. You would be besieged in Orléans still, you and your councils, if I had not made you attack. You believe that this war is a stagnant thing, that it waits for you to be ready – it does not. You don't know how to begin a battle, and I do.

    (She sulks.)

DUNOIS. I know what you think of us, General Joan.

JOAN. And what do you think of me?

DUNOIS. I have not forgotten how the wind changed, and how our hearts changed when you came; and by my faith I shall never deny that it was in your sign that we conquered. But I tell you as a soldier that God is no man's daily drudge, and no maid's either. If you are worthy of it, He will sometimes snatch you out of the jaws of death and set you on your feet again; but that is all: once on your feet you must fight with all your might and all your craft. God set us on our feet through you at Orléans; and the glory of it has carried us through a few good battles here to the coronation. But if we presume on it further, and trust to God to do the work we should do ourselves, we shall be defeated; and serve us right!

JOAN. But –

DUNOIS. *(Interrupting.)* Do not think, any of you, that these victories of ours were won without generalship. I know exactly how much God did for us through The Maid, and how much He left me to do by my own wits. And I tell you that your little hour of miracles is over, and that from this time on he who plays the war game best will win – if luck is on his side.

*(**JOAN** is aghast. **DUNOIS**'s doubt is almost as hurtful as the outright hostility of the others.)*

JOAN. My "little hour of miracles"?

CHARLES. Not content with being Pope Joan, you must be Caesar and Alexander as well.

ARCHBISHOP. Pride will have a fall, Joan.

JOAN. What you call pride is truth and common sense.

DUNOIS. I have learnt the calculous of war. I know how many lives any move of mine will cost; and if the move is worth the cost I make it. But Joan never counts the cost at all: she thinks she has God in her pocket. Up to now she has had the numbers on her side; and she has won. But I know Joan; and I see that someday she will go ahead when she has only ten men to do the work of a hundred. And then she will find that God is on the side of the big battalions.

JOAN. No!

DUNOIS. *(Rounding on her.)* You will! You will be taken by the enemy. And the lucky man that makes the capture will receive sixteen thousand pounds in bounty from the Earl of "Ouareek."

JOAN. Sixteen thousand pounds! Eh, laddie, have they offered that for me? There cannot be so much money in the world.

DUNOIS. There is, in England. And now tell me, all of you, which of you will lift a finger to save Joan once the English have got her?

(Silence descends.)

I speak first, for the army. The day she has been dragged from her horse by a *goddam* and he is not struck dead; the day she is locked in a dungeon, and no angel comes to free her; the day when the enemy finds out that she is as vulnerable as I am and not a bit more invincible... *(He continues quietly, but resolutely.)* she will not be worth the life of a single soldier to us; and I will not risk that life, much as I cherish her as a companion-in-arms.

JOAN. I don't blame you, Jack: you are right. I am not worth one soldier's life if God lets me be beaten. *(Turning to* **CHARLES**.*)* But France may think me worth my ransom after what God has done for her through me.

CHARLES. I tell you I have no money; and this coronation, which is entirely your fault, has cost me all I can borrow.

JOAN. *(Turning to the* **ARCHBISHOP**.*)* The Church is richer than you. I put my trust in the Church.

ARCHBISHOP. Woman: if they get their hands on you, they will drag you through the streets, and burn you as a witch.

JOAN. *(Horrified.)* Oh, my lord, do not say that. It is impossible. I, a witch!

ARCHBISHOP. Peter Cauchon knows his business.

JOAN. But...you would not let them burn me.

ARCHBISHOP. How could I prevent them?

JOAN. You would speak on my behalf. You are a great prince of the Church. I would go anywhere with your blessing to protect me.

ARCHBISHOP. I have no blessing for you while you are proud and disobedient.

JOAN. How can you say that I am disobedient when I always obey my voices?

ARCHBISHOP. The voice of God on earth is the voice of the Church Militant; the voices that come to you are the echoes of your own willfulness.

JOAN. It is not true.

ARCHBISHOP. You tell the Archbishop that he lies; and yet you say you are not proud and disobedient. *(Indignantly.)* It is waste of time admonishing you.

CHARLES. It always comes back to the same thing. She is right, and everyone else is wrong.

ARCHBISHOP. Take this as your last warning. If you perish through setting your private judgment above the instructions of your spiritual directors, the Church will not speak for you. The army will not rescue you. And the throne has not the means to ransom you.

CHARLES. Not a penny.

ARCHBISHOP. You stand alone: absolutely alone. When you pass through these doors into the sunlight, the crowd will cheer you. They will bring you their children and their invalids to heal: they will kiss your hands and feet, poor simple souls, and madden you with the self-confidence that is leading to your destruction. But you will be none the less alone: they cannot save you. We and only we can stand between you and the stake.

DUNOIS. That is the truth, Joan. Heed it.

> (**JOAN** *thinks for a moment, and resolves herself to answer.*)

JOAN. I have better friends and better counsel than yours.

ARCHBISHOP. I see that I am speaking in vain to a hardened heart. You reject our protection, and are determined to turn us all against you. In future, then, fend for yourself. God have mercy on your soul.

> (*The men begin to turn and leave, but* **JOAN** *stops them.*)

JOAN. I thought France would have friends at the court of the king of France; and I find only wolves fighting for pieces of her poor torn body. I thought God would have friends everywhere, because He is the friend of everyone; and in my innocence I believed that you who now cast me out would be like strong towers to keep harm from me. But I am wiser now; and nobody is any the worse for being wiser. Do not think you can frighten me by telling me that I am alone. France is alone; and God is alone; and what is my loneliness before the loneliness of my country and my God? I see now that the loneliness of God is His strength: what would He be if He listened to your jealous little counsels? Well, my loneliness shall be my strength too; it is better to be alone with God; His friendship will not fail me, nor His counsel, nor His love. I will go out now to the common people, and let the love in their eyes comfort me for the hate in yours. You would all be glad to see me burnt; but if I go through the fire I shall go through it to their hearts forever and ever. And so, God be with me!

(She goes from them. They stare after her in glum silence.)

BLUEBEARD. You know, the woman is quite impossible. I don't dislike her, really; but what can one do with such a character?

DUNOIS. I could follow her to hell when the spirit rises in her like that.

ARCHBISHOP. She disturbs my judgment too: there is a dangerous power in her outbursts. But the pit is open at her feet; and for good or evil we cannot turn her from it.

CHARLES. If only she would keep quiet, or go home!

(They follow her dispiritedly. Lights dim.)

Interlude Two – Joan in Prison

(Lights up on a cell in a castle tower of Beaurevoir, June 1430.)

*(***JOAN*** *has been captured by the Burgundians, and she is waiting to be sold to the English, who will try her. She has already been in captivity here for a month. She is ragged and dirty and dispirited – a stark contrast to the last time we saw her in her coronation finery.)*

(She stares out a window of the tower. Offstage we hear men singing an English drinking song[*].)

JOAN. *(Annoyed, putting her hands over her ears.)* Horrible language, English. It sounds like barking.

(Looking out the window.)

It's not so very far down.

*(***ST. CATHERINE*** *and* ***ST. MARGARET*** *appear.)*

You told me, standing at the moat at Melun, that I soon would be taken prisoner, and that I must not be frightened, but accept it willingly. And I begged of you that, when I should be taken, I might die straightaway, without long travail in prison.

ST. CATHERINE. Yes, beloved.

JOAN. Yet I am still locked in this tower, harassed and mocked by faithless Burgundians and *goddams*. I have lost track of the days.

ST. CATHERINE. And it will be many months more, child of God, before you are freed. You must have patience.

---

[*] A license to produce *Saint Joan* does not include a performance license for any third-party or copyrighted music. Licensees should create an original composition or use music in the public domain. For further information, please see Music Use Note on page 3.

JOAN. Patience?! Another thing that would never be asked of a man! Patience, as the English trample back across all the lands that I have won for France! They are undoing my holy work, and worse, while I rot here! Oh, why does Charlie not send for me?

ST. CATHERINE. Charles does not know how to help you without hurting himself. But God has not abandoned you, nor have we. Be of good cheer. You will be freed.

JOAN. When?!

ST. MARGARET. That, we cannot tell you.

JOAN. *(Combative.)* Because you do not know.

ST. MARGARET. *(Flaring.)* Because you do not need to know!

JOAN. And what about the people of Compiègne, where the Burgundians pulled me from my horse and captured me? My guard said that all of the citizens, even the children as young as seven, are to be put to fire and sword. Is that true, or was he lying, to scare me?

ST. MARGARET. All you can do for them now is pray, beloved.

JOAN. I would rather be dead than live on after such destruction of good people! And I would rather be dead than sold to the English, which I know that I am. It is only a matter of time before they collect me, isn't it? And what will I suffer at their hands? I've seen what they do to French women in the villages.

ST. MARGARET. They will not violate you. They will strip you, they will beat you, they will starve you. But that which is consecrated to God will never be defiled.

JOAN. *(Reassured.)* I believe you, Saint Margaret.

(**JOAN** *stares out the window.*)

But again I think: it cannot be that far down.

ST. CATHERINE. Jehanne – do not jump. Please. It is not God's will.

JOAN. They are putting children to the sword! They will put me to the fire!

ST. CATHERINE. God will help you, and the people of Compiègne, too.

JOAN. If God means to help people, I want to be there.

ST. CATHERINE. Do not despair.

JOAN. I don't want to jump out of despair, but out of hope! Hope that I might still be useful, hope to save my own life!

ST. MARGARET. Be patient. Have faith.

JOAN. Faith I have. Patience, I do not. It is a luxury, for people who can see the future. I can see nothing but these walls anymore. And that window.

> *(This is the first time the* **SAINTS** *have told* **JOAN** *the full stories of their deaths.)*

ST. MARGARET. Be obedient, then. As obedient as I was when the Romans tried me, and tortured me, and pushed me into the flames. I would not marry a pagan, I would not renounce my faith, and I terrified my captors the way you terrify yours. But the flames didn't touch me, and the waves could not drown me – I stand on the head of a dragon. God was with me, and he is with you.

ST. CATHERINE. Be obedient as I was, when I converted the philosophers sent to discredit me. My captors led me to the torture chamber. I reached out my hand to the torture wheel, and it shattered at my touch. Have faith.

JOAN. *(Quietly.)* How old were you, when the Romans took your heads?

> *(It is quiet for a moment.)*

ST. MARGARET & ST. CATHERINE. Seventeen.

ST. MARGARET. Earthly death is inevitable, Jehanne. Are we not proof that death is just the beginning of something wonderous?

JOAN. You promised I would be freed!

ST. MARGARET. *(Angrily.)* And you will be! Do you believe us capable of deceit?

JOAN. Perhaps you aren't divine at all! Perhaps you're just the ghosts of stupid girls who came before me! Who got in over their heads and never got out. *(Flaring.)*

Look at me and promise that no harm will come to the people of Compiègne today!

ST. CATHERINE. *(Evenly, divinely calm.)* We can promise you nothing but the salvation of your soul if you follow the will of God.

ST. MARGARET. *(Much less calm than her counterpart.)* Carefully consider your choices, vessel.

(**JOAN** *thinks hard for a moment.*)

JOAN. I cannot beat my fists against these walls any longer. France still needs me.

(**JOAN** *moves to the window, and jumps.*)

Scene Six

(Rouen, 30 May, 1431. A great stone hall in the castle, arranged for a trial – the court being **BISHOP CAUCHON***'s court with the Inquisition participating. There are raised chairs side by side for the Bishop and the Inquisitor. There is a stool for the prisoner.)*

(It is a fine sunshiny May morning.)

*(***LADY WARWICK** *enters, looking for someone. She takes stock of the courtroom for a moment, alone. Then* **CAUCHON** *enters, with the* **INQUISITOR** *and* **D'ESTIVET**.*)*

CAUCHON. I wish your ladyship good-morrow.

LADY WARWICK. Good-morrow to your lordship.

CAUCHON. I suppose your ladyship is aware that you have no business here. This is an ecclesiastical court; you and your husband are only the secular arm.

LADY WARWICK. *(Easily.)* I am aware of that fact. Have I had the pleasure of meeting your friends before? I think not.

CAUCHON. *(Introducing* **THE INQUISITOR**.*)* This, my lady, is Brother John Lemaître, of the order of St. Dominic. He is acting as deputy for the Chief Inquisitor into the evil of heresy in France. Brother John: the Countess of Warwick.

LADY WARWICK. And Worchester. Your Reverence is most welcome. We have no Inquisitor in England, unfortunately; though we miss him greatly.

*(***THE INQUISITOR** *smiles patiently, and bows. He is an austere gentleman, with evident reserves of authority and firmness.)*

CAUCHON. *(Introducing the Canon lawyer.)* This gentleman is Canon John D'Estivet, of the Chapter of Bayeaux. He is acting as Promoter of the Faith.

LADY WARWICK. Promoter?

CAUCHON. Prosecutor, you would call him in civil law.

LADY WARWICK. Ah! Prosecutor. Quite. I am very glad to make your acquaintance, Canon D'Estivet.

> (**D'ESTIVET** *bows. He is well-mannered, but vulpine.*)

May I ask what stage the proceedings have reached? It is now more than nine months since The Maid was captured by the Burgundians. It is very nearly three months since I delivered her up to you, my Lord Bishop. May I suggest that you are taking a rather unconscionably long time to make up your minds? Is this trial never going to end?

THE INQUISITOR. *(Smiling.)* It has not yet begun, my lady.

LADY WARWICK. Not yet begun! Why, you have been at it eleven weeks!

CAUCHON. We have not been idle, my lady. We have held fifteen physical examinations of The Maid: six public and nine private.

LADY WARWICK. And?

D'ESTIVET. We have thoroughly proven that the girl is an intact virgin.

LADY WARWICK. *(Incredulous.)* Is that very important?

D'ESTIVET. It is very important to us!

THE INQUISITOR. *(Always patiently smiling.)* You see, my lady, I have only just decided to associate myself – that is, to associate the Holy Inquisition – with the Bishop's court. I did not at first think that this was a case of heresy at all. I regarded The Maid as a prisoner of war. But having now been present at two of the examinations, I must admit that this seems to be one of the gravest cases of heresy within my experience. Therefore everything is now in order, and we proceed to trial this morning.

LADY WARWICK. *(Graciously.)* Well, that is good news, gentlemen. I will not attempt to conceal from you that our patience was becoming strained.

CAUCHON. *(Sternly.)* I am determined that this woman shall have a fair hearing. The justice of the Church is not a mockery.

THE INQUISITOR. Never has there been a fairer examination within my experience, my lord. The Maid needs no lawyers to take her part: she will be tried by her most faithful friends, all ardently desirous to save her soul from perdition.

D'ESTIVET. Madame: I am the Promotor; and it has been my painful duty to present the case against the girl; but believe me, I would throw up my case today and hasten to her defense if I did not know that my superiors in learning and piety, in eloquence and persuasiveness, have been sent to reason with her, to explain to her the danger she is running, and the ease with which she may avoid it. *(Bursting into lawyerly eloquence.)* Men have dared to say that we are acting from hate, but God is our witness that they lie. Have we tortured her? No. Have we ceased to implore her to have pity on herself, to come to the bosom of her Church as an erring but beloved child? Have we –

LADY WARWICK. *(Interrupting.)* My lord, we certainly do not share your pious desire to save The Maid: her death is a political necessity which I regret but, alas, cannot help. If the Church lets her go –

CAUCHON. *(Interrupting, with fierce pride.)* If the Church lets her go, woe to the man, were he the Emperor himself, who dares lay a finger on her! The Church is not subject to political necessity.

THE INQUISITOR. *(Interposing smoothly.)* You need have no anxiety about the result, my lady. You have an invincible ally in the matter: one who is far more determined than you that she shall burn.

LADY WARWICK. And who is this very convenient partisan, may I ask?

THE INQUISITOR. The Maid herself. She convicts herself ten times over, every time she opens her mouth.

D'ESTIVET. That is perfectly true, my lady. My hair bristles on my head when I hear so young a creature utter such blasphemies.

LADY WARWICK. Well, by all means do your best for her if you are quite sure it will be of no avail.

>   (*Looking hard at* **CAUCHON**.)

We would be sorry to have to act without the blessing of the Church.

CAUCHON. You play for your side, my lady, even at the peril of your soul. I dare not go so far myself. I fear damnation.

LADY WARWICK. If we feared anything we could never govern England, Bishop.

>   (**LADY WARWICK** *turns on her heel and goes out.* **CAUCHON** *takes one of the judicial seats, and* **THE INQUISITOR** *takes the other.* **D'ESTIVET** *studies his brief.*)

>   (**BROTHER LADVENU**, *a young and earnest Dominican, enters.*)

CAUCHON. (*Casually, as he makes himself comfortable.*) What scoundrels these English nobles are!

THE INQUISITOR. All secular power makes men scoundrels. They are not trained for the work, and they have not the Apostolic Succession. Our own French nobles are just as bad.

LADVENU. Inquisitor?

THE INQUISITOR. Yes, Brother Martin?

LADVENU. I come to express grievances from Master de Stogumber and Canon de Courcelles. They are very upset over what you've done to their indictment. They would like me to tell you that they took great pains to draw it up – and they protest that their sixty-four counts have been cut down to twelve.

THE INQUISITOR. In accusing a heretic, as in other things, enough is enough. Twelve will, believe me, be quite enough for our purpose.

*(**CAUCHON** and the **INQUISITOR** share a smirk.)*

I am here as an Inquisitor, not as an ordinary magistrate. We will stick to the heresy, gentlemen; and leave the other matters alone.

LADVENU. Speaking for myself, sir… I wonder if there is any great harm in the girl's heresy? Is it not merely her simplicity? Many saints have said as much as Joan.

THE INQUISITOR. *(Speaking very gravely.)* Brother Martin: if you had seen what I have seen of heresy, you would not think it a light thing. Heresy at first seems innocent and even laudable; but it ends in monstrous horror of unnatural wickedness. For two hundred years the Holy Office has striven with these diabolical madnesses; they begin always by vain and ignorant persons setting up their own judgment against the Church, and taking it upon themselves to be the interpreters of God's will.

You must not fall into the common error of mistaking these simpletons for liars and hypocrites. They believe honestly and sincerely that their diabolical inspiration is divine. Therefore be on your guard against your natural compassion. If you hate evil, remember that nothing is so evil in its consequences as the toleration of heresy.

The work I have to do may seem cruel to those who do not know how much more cruel it would be to leave it undone. I would go to the stake myself sooner than do it if I did not know its righteousness, its necessity, its essential mercy. Have you anything to say, Bishop Cauchon, before we proceed to trial?

CAUCHON. You have spoken for me, and spoken better than I could.

THE INQUISITOR. What provision has the Earl of Warwick made for our defense should The Maid prove obdurate, and the people be moved to pity her?

CAUCHON. The noble earl has eight hundred men-at-arms at the gates. She will not slip through English fingers even if the whole city be on her side.

THE INQUISITOR. God grant that she repent and purge her sin.

CAUCHON. Of course I agree with your lordship.

THE INQUISITOR. *(Calling.)* Let the accused be brought in.

(**JOAN** *enters and walks to the prisoner's stool. She wears a page's black suit. Her long imprisonment and the strain of the examinations which have preceded the trial have left their mark on her, but her vitality still holds. She confronts the court unabashed, without any trace of awe.*)

(*Almost imperceptibly,* **ST. CATHERINE** *and* **ST. MARGARET** *appear on the edges of the courtroom. No one sees them, not even* **JOAN** *at this moment.*)

(Kindly.) You look very pale today. Are you not well?

JOAN. Thank you kindly: I am well enough. But the Bishop sent me some carp; and it made me ill.

CAUCHON. I am sorry. I told them to see that it was fresh.

JOAN. You meant to be good to me, I know. The English thought you were trying to poison me –

CAUCHON. *(Interrupting, to* **THE INQUISITOR.***)* What? No, my Lord.

JOAN. *(Continuing.)* Why do you leave me in the hands of the English? I should be in the hands of the Church. And why must I be chained to my bed? Are you afraid I will fly away?

D'ESTIVET. *(Harshly.)* Woman: it is not for you to question the court: it is for us to question you. When you were left unchained, did you not try to escape by jumping from a tower sixty feet high? If you cannot fly like a witch, how is it that you are still alive?

JOAN. I suppose because the tower was not so high then. It has grown higher every day since you began asking me about it.

D'ESTIVET. Why did you jump from the tower?

JOAN. Why would anybody leave a prison if they could escape? If you leave the door of the cage open, the bird will fly out.

D'ESTIVET. *(Rising.)* That is a confession of heresy. I call the attention of the court to it.

JOAN. Am I a heretic because I try to escape from a prison?

D'ESTIVET. Assuredly, if you are in the hands of the Church, and you willfully take yourself out of its hands, you are deserting the Church, and that is heresy.

JOAN. *(Laughing at him.)* That is nonsense.

D'ESTIVET. You hear, my lord, how I am reviled in the execution of my duty by this woman?

CAUCHON. I have warned you before, Joan, that you are doing yourself no good by these pert answers.

JOAN. But you will not talk sense to me. I am reasonable if you will be reasonable.

THE INQUISITOR. *(Interposing.)* This is not yet in order. You forget, Master Promoter, that the accused has not yet been sworn in on the gospels.

JOAN. I am weary of this argument. I have sworn as much as I will swear. Concerning my father and mother and what I have done since I left home, I will willingly tell all. But the revelations which have come to me from God I have never told or revealed to anyone, except to Charles, my King. Nor would I reveal them if I were to be beheaded.

D'ESTIVET. My lord: she should be put to the torture.

THE INQUISITOR. You hear, Joan? That is what happens to the obdurate. Think before you answer.

JOAN. What more is there to tell that you could understand? If you hurt me, I will say anything you like to stop the pain. But I will take it all back afterwards; so what is the use?

LADVENU. You make a good point. We should proceed mercifully.

D'ESTIVET. But the torture is customary.

THE INQUISITOR. But if the accused will confess voluntarily, its use cannot be justified.

D'ESTIVET. But this is unusual and irregular!

LADVENU. *(Disgusted.)* Do you want to torture the girl for the mere pleasure of it?

D'ESTIVET. *(Bewildered.)* It is not a pleasure. It is the law. It is customary. The woman is a heretic. I assure you it is always done.

CAUCHON. *(Decisively.)* It will not be done today if it is not necessary. Let there be an end of this. I will not have it said that we proceeded on forced confessions.

JOAN. Thou are a rare noodle, Master. Do what was done last time is your rule, eh?

D'ESTIVET. *(Furious.)* Thou wanton: dost thou dare call me noodle?

THE INQUISITOR. Patience, Master, patience: I fear you will soon be only too terribly avenged.

D'ESTIVET. *(Mutters.)* Noodle indeed!

THE INQUISITOR. Meanwhile, let us not be moved by the rough side of a shepherd lass's tongue.

JOAN. Nay: I am no shepherd lass, though I have helped with the sheep like anyone else. I will do a lady's work in the house – spin or weave – against any woman in Rouen.

D'ESTIVET. If you are so clever at woman's work why do you not stay at home and do it?

JOAN. There are plenty of other women to do it, but there is nobody to do my work.

CAUCHON. Come! We are wasting time on trifles. Joan: I am going to put a most solemn question to you. Take care how you answer. Will you promise now to submit yourself to the judgment of God's Church on earth?

JOAN. I am a faithful child of the Church. I will obey the Church –

CAUCHON. *(Interrupting hopefully.)* You will?

JOAN. *(Continuing.)* provided it does not command anything impossible.

> (**CAUCHON** *sinks back with a heavy sigh.* **THE INQUISITOR** *frowns.* **LADVENU** *shakes his head pitifully.)*

If you command me to declare that all that I have done and said, and all the visions and revelations I have had, were not from God – THAT is impossible. I will not declare it for anything in the world. What God made me do I will never go back on. If the Church should bid me do anything contrary to the command I have from God, I will not consent to it.

D'ESTIVET. *(Throwing down his brief.)* Oh! The Church contrary to God! My Lord Inquisitor: do you need anything more than this?

CAUCHON. Woman: you have said enough to burn ten heretics. Will you not be warned? Will you not understand?

THE INQUISITOR. The Church Militant tells you that your revelations and visions are sent by the devil to tempt you to your damnation. Will you not believe that the Church is wiser than you?

JOAN. All the things that you call my crimes – I say that I have done them by the order of God: it is impossible for me to say anything else.

LADVENU. *(Pleading with her urgently.)* You do not know what you are saying, child. Do you want to kill yourself? Listen. Do you not believe that you are subject to the Church of God on earth?

JOAN. God must be served first.

CAUCHON. And you, and not the Church, are to be the judge?

JOAN. What other judgment can I judge by but my own?

> *(The men are scandalized.)*

CAUCHON. Out of your own mouth you have condemned yourself. We have opened the door to you again and

again; and you have shut it in our faces and in the face
of God. Dare you pretend, after what you have said,
that you are in a state of grace?

JOAN. If I am not, may God bring me to it. If I am, may
God keep me in it!

LADVENU. That is a very good reply, my lord.

THE INQUISITOR. What does the Promoter say?

D'ESTIVET. I must emphasize the gravity of two very
horrible and blasphemous crimes which she does
not deny. First, she has intercourse with evil spirits,
and is therefore a sorceress. Second, she wears men's
clothes, which is indecent, unnatural, and abominable;
and in spite of our most earnest remonstrances and
entreaties, she will not change them even to receive the
sacrament.

JOAN. Is the blessed Saint Catherine an evil spirit? Is
Saint Margaret? Is Michael the Archangel, patron of
all France?

D'ESTIVET. How do you know that the spirit which appears
to you is an archangel? Does he appear to you as a
naked man?

JOAN. Do you think God cannot afford to clothe him?

(The assessors cannot help smiling.)

LADVENU. Well answered, Joan.

CAUCHON. Wretched woman! Again I ask you, do you
know what you are saying?

THE INQUISITOR. You wrestle in vain with the devil for her
soul, my lord; she will not be saved. For the last time,
will you put off that impudent attire, and dress as
becomes your sex?

JOAN. I will not.

D'ESTIVET. *(Pouncing.)* The sin of disobedience, my lord.

JOAN. When I have done that for which I am sent from
God, I will put on women's clothing. My voices tell me
that for now, I must dress as a soldier.

LADVENU. Joan, Joan: does not that prove to you that the
voices are the voices of evil spirits? Can you suggest to

us one good reason why an angel of God should give you such shameless advice?

JOAN. Why, yes: what can be plainer common sense? I was a soldier living among soldiers. I am a prisoner guarded by soldiers. If I were to dress as a woman they would think of me as a woman; then what would become of me? If I dress as a soldier they think of me as a soldier, and I can live with them as I do at home with my brothers. That is why Saint Catherine tells me I must not dress as a woman until she gives me leave.

CAUCHON. When will she give you leave?

JOAN. When you take me out of the hands of the English soldiers. Do you want me to live with them in petticoats?

LADVENU. My lord: what she says is, God knows, very shocking, but there is a grain of worldly sense in it such as might impose on a simple village maiden.

JOAN. If we were as simple in the village as you are in your courts and palaces, there would soon be no wheat to make bread for you.

CAUCHON. That is the thanks you get for trying to save her, Brother Martin.

LADVENU. Joan: you are blinded by a terrible pride and self-sufficiency.

JOAN. I have said nothing wrong. I cannot understand.

THE INQUISITOR. It is not enough to be simple. It is not enough even to be what simple people call good. The simplicity of a darkened mind is no better than the simplicity of a beast.

LADVENU. Do you see that man who stands just outside the door?

> (**LADVENU** *indicates the Executioner, a man we cannot see.*)

JOAN. Your torturer? The Bishop said I was not to be tortured.

LADVENU. You do not need to be tortured, because you have confessed everything that is necessary to your condemnation. That man is also the Executioner. He is prepared for the burning of a heretic today. The stake is ready, the wood beneath it is dry. It is all built in the middle of the marketplace. It will be a cruel death.

JOAN. *(Horrified.)* But you are not going to burn me today?

THE INQUISITOR. You realize it at last.

LADVENU. There are eight hundred English soldiers waiting to take you to the marketplace the moment the sentence of excommunication has passed the lips of your judges. You are within a few short moments of that doom.

JOAN. *(Looking around desperately for rescue.)* Oh God! Am I so horribly and cruelly used?! I would rather be beheaded seven times than suffer burning.

LADVENU. Do not despair, Joan. The Church is merciful. You can save yourself.

JOAN. *(Hopefully.)* Yes, my voices promised me I should be freed. Saint Catherine bade me be bold.

CAUCHON. Woman: are you quite mad? Do you not yet see that your voices have deceived you?

JOAN. Oh no: that is impossible.

CAUCHON. Impossible! They have led you straight to your excommunication, and to the fire.

LADVENU. *(Pressing the point hard.)* Have they kept a single promise since you were taken at Compiègne? The devil has betrayed you. The Church holds out its arms to you.

JOAN. I have dared and dared; but only a fool will walk into a fire: God, who gave me my common sense, cannot will me to do that. *(Utterly despairing.)* My voices have deceived me.

LADVENU. God be praised that He has saved you at the eleventh hour!

>   (**LADVENU** *snatches up a sheet of paper, on which he sets to work writing eagerly.)*

CAUCHON. Amen!

JOAN. What must I do?

CAUCHON. You must sign a solemn recantation of your heresy.

D'ESTIVET. *(With growing alarm.)* My lord: do you mean that you are going to allow this woman to escape us?

THE INQUISITOR. The law must take its course, Promotor. You know that.

D'ESTIVET. I know what the Earl of Warwick will do when he learns that we intend to betray him. There are eight hundred men at the gate who will see that this abominable witch is burnt in spite of this court's decision. You have been doing nothing but begging this slut on your knees to recant all through this trial.

THE INQUISITOR. Silence! Gentlemen: pray silence! Master D'Estivet: bethink you a moment of your holy office: of what you are, and where you are. I direct you to sit down.

> *(***D'ESTIVET*** sits, angry and scared of how the English will react to this acquittal.)*

LADVENU. *(With the paper in his hand.)* My lord: here is the form of recantation for The Maid to sign.

CAUCHON. Read it to her, Brother Martin. And let all be silent.

> *(During the reading of this confession, ***ST. CATHERINE*** and ***ST. MARGARET*** come forward. ***JOAN*** sees them now, but still feels they have abandoned her. They stand far from her.)*

LADVENU. *(Reading quietly.)* "I, Joan, commonly called The Maid, a miserable sinner, do confess that I have most grievously sinned in the following articles."

ST. CATHERINE. Do not trust them, Jehanne.

LADVENU. "I have pretended to have revelations from God and the angels and the blessed saints, and perversely rejected the Church's warnings that these were temptations by demons."

ST. MARGARET. Their mercy is a trap.

LADVENU. "I have blasphemed abominably by wearing an immodest dress, contrary to the Holy Scripture and the canons of the Church. I have worn my hair in the style of a man, and, against all the duties which have made my sex specially acceptable in heaven, have taken up the sword, even inciting men to slay each other."

ST. CATHERINE. Have faith, beloved. Do not commit this treason.

LADVENU. "I confess to the sin of idolatry, to the sin of disobedience, to the sin of pride, and to the sin of heresy."

ST. MARGARET. You are damning your soul to save your body!

LADVENU. "All of which sins I now renounce and depart from, humbly thanking you Doctors and Masters who have brought me back into the grace of our Lord. All this I swear by God Almighty and the Holy Gospels, in witness whereto I sign my name to this recantation."

ST. MARGARET & ST. CATHERINE. Stay the course. You are never alone.

JOAN. Everyone has abandoned me!

ST. MARGARET & ST. CATHERINE. Act, and God will act.

(JOAN *is distracted by the voices.*)

THE INQUISITOR. (*Calling her back.*) You understand this, Joan?

JOAN. It is plain enough, sir.

THE INQUISITOR. And is it true?

(JOAN *stares at her voices for a long moment before responding.*)

JOAN. If it were not true, the fire would not be ready for me in the market-place.

LADVENU. (*Going to her quickly lest she should compromise herself again.*) Come, child: let me guide your hand. Take the pen.

(They begin to write, using the book as a desk.)

(He pronounces the letters in French, then the name in English.) J-O-A-N. "Joan." So. Now make your mark by yourself.

JOAN. My name is Jehanne.

LADVENU. The English will never be able to pronounce that. To them, you must be "Joan."

JOAN. Is even my name to be taken from me now?

> *(***JOAN*** makes her mark, defeated, then gives him back the pen and paper, tormented by the rebellion of her mind against her soul.)*

There!

LADVENU. Praise be to God, my brothers, the lamb has returned to the flock! And the shepherd rejoices in her more than in ninety and nine just persons.

THE INQUISITOR. *(Taking the paper.)* We declare thee by this act set free from the danger of excommunication in which you stood. You will not die today.

JOAN. I thank you.

THE INQUISITOR. But because you have sinned most presumptuously against God and the Holy Church, and so that you may repent your errors in solitary contemplation, and be shielded from all temptation to return to them, we, for the good of thy soul, do condemn you to perpetual imprisonment to the end of thy earthly days.

JOAN. *(Rising in terrible anger.)* Perpetual imprisonment! Am I not then to be set free?

LADVENU. Set free, child, after such wickedness as yours! What are you dreaming of?

JOAN. Give me that writing.

> *(***JOAN*** snatches up the paper and tears it into fragments.)*

You promised me my life; but you lied. You think that life is nothing but not being stone dead. I could live on bread and water; I could do without my warhorse; I could drag about in a skirt; I could let the banners and the trumpets and the knights and soldiers pass me and leave me behind as they leave the other women. But to shut me from the light of the sky and the sight of the fields and flowers? To chain my feet so that I can never again climb the hills? To make me breathe foul damp darkness, and keep from me everything that brings me back to the love of God when your wickedness tempts me to hate Him? No. Without these things I cannot live; and by your wanting to take them away from me, or any human creature, I know that your counsel is of the devil, and that mine is of God. Light your fire: do you think I dread it as much as the life of a rat in a hole? I would rather be dead than useless.

D'ESTIVET. Blasphemy! Blasphemy! She is possessed. She is a relapsed heretic, obstinate, incorrigible, and altogether unworthy of the mercy we have shown her. I call for her excommunication. *(Calling through the door.)* Light your fire, Executioner!

LADVENU. You wicked girl: if your counsel were of God, would He not deliver you?

JOAN. His ways are not your ways. I will not deny the miracle that I am in order to comfort you in your smallness. I will not make myself less so that you can be more. I would rather die. I give myself back to myself. *(Pause, then calmer.)* You believe that you are my judges. Take thought over what you are doing. Truly, you will not do harm to me without suffering for it both in body and soul. That is my last word to you.

D'ESTIVET. Seize her!

CAUCHON. Not yet.

> *(They wait. There is a dead silence.* **CAUCHON** *turns to* **THE INQUISITOR** *with an inquiring look.* **THE INQUISITOR** *nods affirmatively. They rise solemnly and intone the sentence antiphonally.)*

We decree that you are a relapsed heretic.

THE INQUISITOR. Cast out from the unity of the Church.

CAUCHON. Sundered from her body.

THE INQUISITOR. Infected with the leprosy of heresy.

CAUCHON. A member of Satan.

> (*At this,* **JOAN** *nearly swoons, but her* **VOICES** *step in and support her, unseen by the men.*)

THE INQUISITOR. We declare that you must be excommunicate.

CAUCHON. And now we do cast thee out, segregate thee, and abandon thee to the secular power.

D'ESTIVET. Into the fire with the witch.

> (**D'ESTIVET** *rushes at her and forces her out of the room.* **ST. MARGARET** *and* **ST. CATHERINE** *stay with her.*)

THE INQUISITOR. That man is an incorrigible fool.

CAUCHON. Brother Martin: see that everything is done in order.

LADVENU. My place is at her side, my lord.

> (**LADVENU** *hurries after them.*)

CAUCHON. (*Anxiously.*) These English are impossible: they will thrust her straight into the fire without a secular hearing. (*Turning to go.*) We must stop that.

THE INQUISITOR. (*Calmly.*) Yes; but not too fast, my lord. We have proceeded in perfect order. If the English choose to put themselves in the wrong, it is not our business to put them in the right. And the sooner it is over, the better for that poor girl.

CAUCHON. (*Relaxing.*) That is true. I suppose we must see this dreadful thing through.

THE INQUISITOR. One gets used to it. Habit is everything. I am accustomed to the fire: it is soon over. But it is a terrible thing to see a young and innocent creature crushed between these mighty forces, the Church and the Law.

CAUCHON. You call her innocent!

THE INQUISITOR. Oh, quite innocent. What does she know? She did not understand a word we were saying. Come, or we shall be late for the end.

>*(They are going out when* **LADY WARWICK** *comes in, meeting them.)*

LADY WARWICK. Oh, I am intruding. I thought it was all over.

CAUCHON. It is all over, my lady.

THE INQUISITOR. The execution is not in our hands, but it is desirable that we should witness the end. So by your leave –

>*(***THE INQUISITOR** *bows and exits.)*

CAUCHON. There is some doubt whether your people have observed the forms of law, my lady.

LADY WARWICK. I am told that there is some doubt whether your authority runs in this city, my lord. However, if you will answer for that I will swear for the rest.

CAUCHON. It is to God that we both must answer. Good morning, my lady.

LADY WARWICK. My lord: good morning.

>*(They look at one another for a moment with unconcealed hostility. Then* **CAUCHON** *follows* **THE INQUISITOR** *out.)*

>*(***LADY WARWICK** *looks round and finds herself alone.)*

LADY WARWICK. *(Silence.)* Hallo, there! *(Silence.)* They have all gone to see the burning.

>*(Brother* **LADVENU** *enters, slowly. He is as white as a sheet, as if he's seen a ghost.)*

LADY WARWICK. What in the devil's name – ?

LADVENU. My lady, my lady: for Christ's sake pray for my wretched guilty soul. I am not a bad man, my lady.

LADY WARWICK. No, no: not at all.

LADVENU. I meant no harm. I did not know what it would be like.

LADY WARWICK. *(Hardening.)* Oh! You saw it, then?

LADVENU. I did not know what I was doing, and I shall be damned to all eternity for it.

LADY WARWICK. Nonsense! Very distressing, no doubt; but it was not your doing.

LADVENU. I let them do it. If I had known, I would have torn her from their hands. We madden ourselves with words. But when it is brought home to you; when you see the thing you have done; when it is blinding your eyes, stifling your nostrils, tearing your heart, then – then –

(Falling on his knees.)

O God, take away this sight from me! She is in Thy bosom; and I am in hell forevermore.

LADY WARWICK. *(Hauling him to his feet.)* Come, come, man! Pull yourself together. If you don't have the nerve to see these things, why did you not stay away?

LADVENU. I took this cross from the church for her that she might see it at the end: she had only two sticks tied together that a soldier had given her. When the fire crept round us, she warned me to get down and save myself. My lady: a girl who could think of another's danger in such a moment was not inspired by the devil. When I had to snatch the cross from her sight, she looked up to heaven. And I do not believe that the heavens were empty. This is not the end for her, but the beginning. I will go pray among her ashes. I am no better than Judas.

LADY WARWICK. There will be no ashes. I have seen to it that there will be no relics to sell. Not a bone, not a nail, not a hair. Everything left of her will be thrown into the river. We have heard the last of Joan.

LADVENU. The last of her? Oh no, my lady. Not at all.

(Lights dim on the courtroom.)

Epilogue

(Paris, July 1456 – twenty-five years after **JOAN***'s execution.)*

*(***KING CHARLES VII** *of France, formerly* **JOAN***'s Dauphin, now* **CHARLES** *the Victorious, is reading in bed in his royal chateau.)*

(A distant clock strikes the half-hour softly. **LADVENU** *enters, older, strange and stark in bearing, and still carrying the cross from Rouen.* **CHARLES** *springs out of bed.)*

LADVENU. *(Solemnly.)* I bring you glad tidings of great joy. Justice, long delayed, is at last triumphant.

CHARLES. *(Jumping out of bed.)* Brother Martin! Is it over?

LADVENU. *(Looking at the cross in his hand.)* I held this cross when The Maid perished in the fire. Twenty-five years have passed since then: nearly ten thousand days. And on every one of those days I have prayed to God to justify His daughter on earth as she is justified in heaven.

CHARLES. *(Impatient.)* Yes, yes, everyone knows you have a bee in your bonnet about The Maid. Have you been at the inquiry?

LADVENU. I have given my testimony. It is over.

CHARLES. Satisfactorily?

LADVENU. At her first trial, the truth was told; the law was upheld; mercy was shown beyond all custom, and in the end a saint was sent to the stake as a sorceress.

CHARLES. And?

LADVENU. This new trial, from which I have just come, was an orgy of lying and foolishness. And yet, the result is that a great lie is silenced forever; and a great wrong is set right before all men. She is vindicated. The ways of God are very strange.

CHARLES. My friend: if they can no longer say that I was crowned by a witch and a heretic, I shall not fuss about how the trick has been done. Is her posthumous rehabilitation complete?

LADVENU. It is solemnly declared that her judges were full of corruption, fraud, and malice. All lies.

CHARLES. Never mind the lies: her judges are dead.

LADVENU. The sentence on her is annulled.

CHARLES. Good. Nobody can challenge my coronation now, can they?

LADVENU. Not Charlemagne nor King David himself was more sacredly crowned.

CHARLES. Excellent. Think of what that means to me!

LADVENU. I think of what it means to her.

CHARLES. You cannot. None of us ever knew what anything meant to her. She was like nobody else; and she must take care of herself wherever she is; for *I* cannot take care of her; and neither can you, whatever you may think: you are not big enough. But I will tell you this about her. If you could bring her back to life, they would burn her again within six months, for all their present adoration of her. And you would hold up the cross, too, just the same. So let her rest; and let you and I mind our own business, and not meddle with hers.

LADVENU. *(Quietly.)* From now on my path will not lie through palaces, nor my conversation be with kings.

(**LADVENU** *exits. A moment passes.*)

(*Then: Thunder. Lightening. The candles go out.* **JOAN**, **ST. CATHERINE**, *and* **ST. MARGARET** *enter the room.*)

CHARLES. Hallo! Someone come and shut the windows: everything is being blown all over the place.

(*A light appears and* **CHARLES** *dimly sees a figure.*)

Who's there? Who's there? Help! Murder!

JOAN. Easy, Charlie, easy. What are you making all that noise for? No one can hear you. It's just us here.

CHARLES. Us?

JOAN. You, me, Saint Catherine, Saint Margaret.

CHARLES. I don't see them.

JOAN. Even now, Charlie? Well, they often come among
Christian people and are not seen. I saw them many
times among Christians.

CHARLES. Joan! Are you a ghost, Joan?

JOAN. Hardly even that. Can a poor burnt-up lass have a
ghost?

(She stares at him.)

You look older, Charlie.

CHARLES. I am older. Am I asleep?

JOAN. No, but not really awake, either.

CHARLES. That's funny.

JOAN. Not so funny as that I am dead, is it?

CHARLES. Are you really dead? Amazing! Did it hurt much?
Being burnt?

JOAN. Oh, that! I cannot remember very well. I think it did
at first; but then it all got mixed up; and I was not in my
right mind until I was free of the body. But I certainly
don't recommend it. How have you been ever since?

CHARLES. Oh, not so bad. Do you know, I actually lead my
army out and win battles? Down into the moat up to
my waist in mud and blood. Up the ladders with the
stones and hot pitch raining down. Like you.

JOAN. No! Did I make a man of you after all, Charlie?

CHARLES. I am Charles the Victorious now. I have had to
be rough and brave. The people expected it, after you.

JOAN. I was always a rough one: a regular soldier. I might
almost have been a man. Pity I wasn't: I should not
have bothered you all so much then.

ST. CATHERINE. The glory of God was upon you, Jehanne.
Your head was in the skies.

ST. MARGARET. Man or woman, you would have bothered
them as long as their noses were in the mud.

JOAN. Now tell us, what has happened since you wise men knew no better than to make a heap of cinders of me?

CHARLES. Your mother and brothers have sued the courts to have your case tried over again. And the courts have declared that your judges were full of fraud and malice. The sentence on you is broken, annulled.

JOAN. Can they unburn me as well?

CHARLES. If they could, they would think twice before they did it. But they have decreed that a beautiful cross be placed where the stake stood, for your perpetual memory and for your salvation.

ST. MARGARET. It is the memory and the salvation that sanctify the cross, not the other way around.

ST. CATHERINE. Your memory will outlast that cross.

JOAN. I shall be remembered when men have forgotten where Rouen stood.

CHARLES. There you go with your self-conceit, the same as ever! I think you might say a word of thanks to me for having had justice done at last.

(**CAUCHON** *appears.*)

CAUCHON. Justice?! You liar!

JOAN. Why, if it isn't Bishop Cauchon! How are you, Peter? What luck have you had since you burned me?

CAUCHON. None!

JOAN. But what has happened to you? Are you dead or alive?

CAUCHON. Dead. Dishonored. They pursued me beyond the grave. They excommunicated my dead body: they dug it up and flung it into the common sewer.

JOAN. Your dead body did not feel the sewer as my live body felt the fire.

CAUCHON. But this thing that they have done against me hurts justice. Wrongs should not be undone by slandering the pure of heart.

JOAN. Well, well, Peter, I hope men will be the better for remembering me; and they would not remember me so well if you had not burned me.

CAUCHON. Their courage will rise as they think of you, only to faint as they think of me. Yet God is my witness: I could do no other than I did.

CHARLES. Yes: it is always you good men that do the big mischiefs. Look at me! I am not Charles the Good, nor Charles the Wise, nor Charles the Bold. Joan's worshippers even call me Charles the Coward because I did not pull her out of the fire. But I have done less harm than any of you. And I ask you, what king of France has done better, or been a better fellow in his own little way?

JOAN. Are you really king of France, Charlie? Are the English gone?

(**DUNOIS** *enters.*)

DUNOIS. I have kept my word: the English are gone.

JOAN. Praised be God! Tell me all about the fighting, Jack. Was it you that led them? Were you God's captain even unto death?

DUNOIS. I am not dead. My body is very comfortably asleep in my bed at Châteaudun.

ST. CATHERINE. His spirit is called here by yours.

JOAN. And you fought them <u>my</u> way, Jack? Not the old way, but The Maid's way: fighting for peace, with the heart high and humble and void of malice? Was it my way, Jack?

DUNOIS. Faith, it was any way that would win. But the way that won was always <u>your</u> way. I thought of you in every battle, Joan. I should never have let the priests burn you; but I was busy fighting; and it was the Church's business, not mine. There was no use in both of us being burned, was there?

CAUCHON. Ay! Put the blame on the priests. The Church Militant sent this woman to the fire; but even as she burned, the flames whitened into the radiance of the Church Triumphant.

JOAN. If that is true, it happened in spite of your efforts, not because of them.

ST. CATHERINE. It is true, beloved.

ST. MARGARET. Look, another visitor.

(**LADY WARWICK** *enters.*)

LADY WARWICK. Madam: my congratulations on your rehabilitation. I feel that I owe you an apology.

JOAN. Oh, please don't mention it.

LADY WARWICK. (*Pleasantly.*) The burning was purely political. There was no personal feeling against you, I assure you.

JOAN. I bear no malice, my lady.

LADY WARWICK. Just so. Very kind of you to say: a touch of true breeding. But I must insist on apologizing very amply. The truth is, these political necessities sometimes turn out to be political mistakes; and this one was a veritable howler. For your spirit conquered us, madam, in spite of our fire. Still, when they make you a saint, you will owe your halo to me.

JOAN. I shall owe nothing to any of you: I owe everything to the spirit of God within me. But fancy me a saint!

(*Turning to her* **VOICES.**)

What would the two of you say if the farm girl was cocked up beside you?

(**ST. CATHERINE** *and* **ST. MARGARET** *smile at her.*)

(*A* **MESSENGER** *arrives. He is an upright cleric, dressed in the clothing of a priest from the 1920s. He arrives from* **JOAN***'s canonization trial. They all stare at him. Then they burst into uncontrollable laughter.*)

THE MESSENGER. Why this mirth, gentlemen?

LADY WARWICK. I congratulate you on having invented a most extraordinarily comic dress.

THE MESSENGER. I do not understand. You are all in fancy dress: I am properly dressed. In any case, I am here

on serious business, and cannot engage in frivolous
discussions.

> *(He takes out a paper, and assumes a dry
> official manner.)*

I am sent to announce to you that Joan of Arc, formerly
known as The Maid, having been the subject of an
inquiry instituted by the Bishop of Orléans –

JOAN. *(Interrupting.)* Ah! They remember me still in
Orléans.

THE MESSENGER. *(Continuing.)* into the claim of said Joan
of Arc to be canonized as a saint –

JOAN. *(Again interrupting.)* But I never made any such
claim.

THE MESSENGER. *(Continuing emphatically.)* The Church
has examined the claim exhaustively in the usual
course, and has finally declared her to have been
endowed with heroic virtues and favored with private
revelations, and calls her to the communion of the
Church Triumphant as Saint Joan.

JOAN. *(In disbelief.)* Saint Joan!

THE MESSENGER. On every thirtieth day of May, being
the anniversary of the death of the said most blessed
daughter of God, there shall in every Catholic church
to the end of time be celebrated a special office in
commemoration of her. And it shall be lawful and
laudable for the faithful to kneel and address their
prayers through her to the Mercy Seat.

JOAN. Oh no. It is for the saint to kneel.

> *(She falls on her knees, rapt.)*

THE MESSENGER. In Basilica Vaticana, the sixteenth day of
May, nineteen hundred and twenty.

DUNOIS. *(Raising JOAN.)* Half an hour to burn you, dear
saint, and four centuries to find out the truth!

> *(ST. CATHERINE waves her hand, and they all
> stare at a vision of the future that is conjured.
> A statue of JOAN on a horse.)*

JOAN. Is that statue meant to be me? I am glad they have not forgotten my horse.

CHARLES. That is Rheims Cathedral where you had me crowned. It must be you.

ST. CATHERINE. And there are thousands more like it, all across creation.

JOAN. But who has broken my sword? My sword was never broken. It is the sword of France.

DUNOIS. Never mind. Swords can be mended. Your soul is unbroken; and you are the soul of France.

(The vision fades.)

JOAN. My sword shall conquer yet: the sword that never struck a blow. Though men destroyed my body, yet in my soul I have seen God.

(Something occurs to her. She turns excitedly to **ST. CATHERINE** *and* **ST. MARGARET**.*)*

I am a saint! And saints can work miracles! And now tell me: shall I rise from the dead, and come back to earth a living woman?

(Everyone murmurs in consternation. **ST. CATHERINE** *and* **ST. MARGARET** *look apologetic, but serene.)*

What! Must I burn again? Are none of you ready to receive me?

CAUCHON. Mortal eyes cannot distinguish the saint from the heretic. Spare them.

*(***CAUCHON*** exits.)*

DUNOIS. Forgive us, Joan: we are not yet good enough for you. Your return would not make me the man you once thought me. Though I dare not bless you, I hope I may one day enter into your blessedness. Meanwhile, however, I shall go back to my bed.

*(***DUNOIS*** exits.)*

LADY WARWICK. We sincerely regret our little mistake; but political necessities, though occasionally erroneous, are

still imperative; so if you will be good enough to excuse
me...

> (**LADY WARWICK** *exits.*)

THE MESSENGER. The possibility of your resurrection
was not contemplated in the recent proceedings for
your canonization. I must return to Rome for fresh
instructions.

> (**THE MESSENGER** *bows and exits.*)

CHARLES. Oh, do not come back: you must not come back.
I must die in peace. Give us peace in our time, O Lord!

> (**CHARLES** *flees the room.*)

JOAN. *(Sadly.)* Goodbye, Charlie.

> (**JOAN** *turns to her voices. The three teenage
> virgin martyrs are alone onstage.*)

And you, my faithful companions? What words of
comfort have you for Saint Joan now?

ST. CATHERINE. When they pray to you, you will hear them
and intercede. Even these.

ST. MARGARET. You are more use to them in Paradise than
on earth.

JOAN. I just wish they understood!

ST. CATHERINE. It lies with our Lord to make revelations to
whom he pleases.

ST. MARGARET. If those who ask for understanding are not
worthy enough to receive it, we are not accountable for
that.

JOAN. O God that madest this beautiful earth, when will it
be ready to receive Thy saints? How long, O Lord, how
long?

> (*Lights dim on the saints.*)

> (*Blackout.*)

End of Play

Appendix – Timeline of Historical Events

~287 AD	Saint Catherine of Alexandria born in Alexandria, Egypt to a prosperous family.
289 AD	Saint Margaret of Antioch born in Antioch, Turkey. She is the daughter of a pagan priest, and when she converts to Christianity, she is driven from her home by her father.
301 AD	At age fourteen, Catherine has a vision of the Blessed Virgin Mary and the Baby Jesus, and converts to Christianity.
~303 AD	Olybrius, Roman Governor of Antioch, asks to marry Margaret when she is fourteen years old. He demands that she renounce Christianity. Because she has consecrated her virginity to God, Margaret refuses. Olybrius has her arrested, imprisoned, and tortured.
304 AD	While in prison, Margaret is visited by Satan in the form of a dragon. He swallows her, but the cross she carries irritates his intestines and the dragon spits her out. The next day, attempts are made to execute her by fire and drowning, but she is miraculously saved and converts thousands of spectators. Finally, she is beheaded.
	Roman Emperor Maxentius begins persecuting Christians. Catherine denounces his cruelty. Maxentius calls together fifty male orators and philosophers to debate her. However, Catherine speaks movingly in defense of her beliefs. She is so persuasive that several people present convert to Christianity, including the Emperor's wife.
305 AD	Catherine is imprisoned. An attempt is made to torture her, but the breaking wheel shatters at her touch (and is afterward known as The Catherine Wheel). She is then beheaded.

***

April 1337	The "Hundred Years' War" begins between England and France.
January 6, 1412	Joan is believed to have been born on this date in Domrémy, Lorraine, France. She is soon after baptized.

October 1415	Henry V of England wins a key victory over the French in Normandy in the Battle of Agincourt. Many French noblemen die in the fighting and Charles, Duke of Orléans is taken prisoner by the English.
July 1416	King Henry of England and John the Fearless of Burgundy (French) enter into a treaty in which they promise not to wage war against each other in the Duke of Orléans's northern territories.
January 1418	Burgundian troops invade and capture Rouen, the capital of Normandy. Meanwhile, English forces seize control of other French territories.
January 1419	English forces take Rouen and move toward Paris.
September 10, 1419	Armagnac supporters of the Dauphin Charles (French) lure John the Fearless of Burgundy to a bridge at Montereau, for what he believes will be a diplomatic meeting. Instead, he is assassinated. This ends all hope of an Armagnac-Burgundian alliance against the English.
May 21, 1420	Duke Philip of Burgundy (French) and the English enter into a treaty. King Charles VI (French) recognizes Henry King of England, his son-in-law, as the rightful heir to the French throne. This bypasses King Charles VI's own son, the Dauphin Charles (French), and his heirs.
January 6, 1421	The Dauphin Charles (French) is summoned to answer charges in Paris, relating to the death of John the Fearless. He does not appear.
August 31, 1422	King Henry V (English) dies.
October 21, 1422	King Charles VI (French) dies. John the Duke of Bedford (English) is named regent of France on behalf of Henry's nine-month-old son.
1425	Joan begins to hear voices at age thirteen.
May 1428	Joan's kinsman, Durand Laxart, who believes that she has been given a holy mission, takes her to the nearest French stronghold at Vaucouleurs, which is under the command of Captain Robert de Baudricourt. Joan asks to join the Dauphin Charles's (French) forces, and is turned away.
Fall 1428	The English begin their long siege of Orléans, a town on the river Loire. This river forms the border between Dauphinist France to the south, and English/Burgundian France to the north.

January 1429	Joan again attempts to join Charles's (French) forces at Vaucouleurs. She is permitted to join up on this second attempt.
February 13, 1429	Joan leaves Vaucouleurs dressed in a male soldier's clothing. She goes to Chinon, where the Dauphin Charles (French) and his court are staying. Joan asks to help fight the English and the Burgundians. Charles has her interrogated by Catholic clergymen for three weeks.
April 1429	Satisfied with her piety, Dauphin Charles gives Joan command of a small military force. On her way to join the fight at Orléans, she sends a representative to the church of Sainte Catherine de Fierbois, to retrieve a sword her voices say will be waiting for her there. The sword is found.
April 29, 1429	Joan and her troops reach Orléans and meet Jean de Dunois (French), first cousin of the Dauphin and leader of the French defenses. They are told to wait for reinforcements.
May 4, 1429	Acting on divine inspiration, Joan leads an attack on the English.
May 7–8, 1429	Though she is wounded in battle, Joan and her troops force the English to abandon their siege of Orléans, which had been going on for two hundred and ten days.
May 9, 1429	Joan joins the royal court at Tours, where she tells the Dauphin Charles (French) he must go immediately to Reims and be crowned in the cathedral there. Reims is under British control.
June 18, 1429	Joan's army defeats the English army at the Battle of Patay.
June 17, 1429	The people of Reims welcome the Dauphin and Joan, throwing up open the gates of the city to them, in spite of the city's British occupation. Negotiations take place. The day after Joan and her army enter Reims, Charles VII is crowned King of France at Reims Cathedral.
July 20, 1429	Charles leaves Reims and parades around the region for a month, before retreating to Loire.
August 28, 1429	Burgundy and France sign a four-month truce.
September 8, 1429	Joan's army attacks Paris. Joan is shot by a crossbow bolt, and her troops withdraw.
December 1429	Charles bestows nobility status upon Joan, her parents, and her two brothers, who had both fought alongside her at Orléans.

May 14, 1430	Joan reaches Compiègne, where the French troops are vastly outnumbered by the attacking Burgundian forces. Joan holds off the Burgundians as long as she can, while French citizens escape the city.
May 23, 1430	Joan is captured by Burgundian troops at Compiègne. She is considered a more valuable prize than the city itself.
May 25, 1430	Paris learns of Joan's capture.
~July 1430	While imprisoned at Beaurevoir Castle, Joan makes several escape attempts. In one instance, she jumps from a seventy-foot tower, landing in a dry moat. After this, she is moved to the Burgundian town of Arras.
November 1430	For a price, the Burgundians turn Joan over to the English.
January 3, 1431	Joan is transferred to the church for interrogation. Pierre Cauchon, Bishop of Beauvais, will oversee the interrogation, since Joan was captured in his diocese.
January 9, 1431	Joan's trial begins. Representatives of the court are sent to her home village of Domrémy, to inquire about her life and history. Nothing is found in these inquiries to support the charges against her.
February 21, 1431	Joan is brought before the court, and the first of six public examinations is held. Joan is given no representative and must defend herself against theologians and canon lawyers.
March 3, 1431	Public court examinations of Joan end. Private examinations of Joan in her cell begin. These will total fifteen sessions.
March 26, 1431	Joan's regular trial begins with the reading of seventy articles of accusation and Joan's responses to each. These seventy accusations are later summarized into a twelve-article indictment.
May 23, 1431	Joan is found guilty on each of the twelve articles of the indictment.
May 24, 1431	Joan is sentenced to death. She is told that she will be burned immediately, unless she agrees to stop wearing men's clothing, and signs a document in which she renounces her visions. Joan, frightened, signs this last-minute abjuration.

May 29, 1431	After five days in prison, Joan once again puts on men's clothing, and rescinds her abjuration. The church declares her a relapsed heretic, a transgression punishable by execution. She is transferred from the custody of the church to the custody of the British government.
May 30, 1431	Joan is burned at the stake in the Old Marketplace at Rouen.

***

November 1449	French forces retake Rouen.
February 13, 1450	Charles VII (formerly Charles the Dauphin) authorizes an inquiry into Joan's trial of condemnation, under public pressure from her supporters. He has a valid reason to want her name cleared. Joan crowned Charles VII – if she was a heretic, his coronation can be considered tainted.
May 1452	Inquisitor-General Jean Brehal, after an examination of Joan's case, recommends an appeal of her verdict.
November 7, 1455	In Nôtre-Dame Cathedral in Paris, Joan's mother and two brothers petition the Pope for a revision of her sentence, restoration of her honor, and the examination of her judges from the 1431 trial. Pope Calixtus III approves this new trial and appoints judges.
December 12, 1455	The "Nullification Trial" officially opens in Paris. Some one hundred and fifteen witnesses testify to Joan's courage, integrity, and purity. Witnesses include childhood friends, soldiers who served with her, citizens she saved, and some of the tribunal members who had interrogated her in 1431.
July 7, 1456	The Nullification Trial concludes with the finding that Joan was innocent and wrongfully executed. The original trial is declared "tainted with fraud [...] and manifest errors of fact and law." Joan's elderly mother lives to see the final verdict read and her daughter's name cleared.

***

May 16, 1920	Joan is canonized as a saint by Pope Benedict XV.